CM DOPORTO

OPPOSING SIDES

UNIVERSITY PARK SERIES BOOK 1

Opposing Sides
Book 1 from
The University Park Series
By CM Doporto

Diane –
Live.
Laugh.
Read.

CM Doporto

Acknowledgements

I'd like to thank my husband for his continual support. I can't do this without you babe. To my son, for allowing me to write when I should be playing with you.

A huge shout out to my critique partner, Sam. Your help has been wonderful, and I'm glad we work well together. Many thanks to my street team, CM Doporto's Heroes and Heroines. I appreciate your dedication and time with supporting my books and getting the word out. A big thank you to Smexy Fab Four for managing my team and getting things back on track for me. Monica, Sheri and Jessa for editing the book for me. You know I'm not perfect. Thanks to Cora Graphics for creating another beautiful cover!

I would be remiss if I didn't mention the bloggers and reviewers who take the time to read and post reviews. Your support of indie authors helps get the attention of readers we work hard to obtain.

A huge thank you to you, the reader. Without you there would be no one to read my story. I appreciate you taking the time to read it. I hope you enjoy it as much as I did writing it.

Most of all I want to thank our Heavenly Father for providing me with the opportunity to do what I love, write.

Dedication

To my mom.
Thank you for not being a helicopter parent.
I love you.

Chapter 1

"Lexi, are you okay?" Delaney snapped a picture that broke me from my incoherent gaze.

"Yes, I'm fine." I forced a smile to my roommate and good friend since junior year.

"Just thinking of everything that needs to be done in the next few months."

"Oh, sweetie. I don't want you stressing yourself over the details," Mom said, squeezing a hug from behind. "That's why we hired Melissa, remember? The wedding planner is there to handle all of that so you don't have to worry."

I huffed out a breath. "I know, but it's still a lot that I have to manage and with school—"

"Lexi, if there is anything you need, just say the word." My soon to be mother-in-law, Suzanne, gave me a thorough look over. "That dress is absolutely perfect! Collin will be speechless." She pressed a hand to her chest as her eyes glazed over with tears.

"Oh, I couldn't agree more." Mom fluffed the back of the A-line style dress that had lace up to my neck.

I pulled on the neckline, gasping for air. "I actually like the other one better." I said, pointing to a strapless ball gown with an organza-ruffled skirt that had a sequined bodice. "This one has too much lace."

"Oh, but it's beautiful." Mom lifted my arms, continuing to admire the dress made for a conservative young female. After all, that was who I was supposed to be. "The other one shows too much skin." She took my fairytale dress and handed it to the sales lady. "We will pass on this one."

"But what if I wore a jacket? I'm sure Pastor Clifton would be okay with it."

"I think my husband would agree that the dress you have on is more suitable. Olivia, what do you think Lexi's dad would say? I mean…" Suzanne continued to ramble with my mother about the wedding dress they had chosen for me. Yes, that's correct. The one they chose, not me.

Sadly, I couldn't picture myself walking down the aisle in it. Aside from hating it, I had serious reservations about saying 'I do'. It felt like Collin and I were marrying to appease our parents instead of marrying for love. We had known each other since we were thirteen and had been together for the past four years. Everyone expected us to take that next step. So, when he asked for my hand, I naturally accepted.

"Lex, seriously girl, what's up with you?" Delaney continued clicking her camera from different angles, demanding my attention.

"Like I said, I have a lot on my mind. Mid-terms are approaching and so is the wedding."

She cast a doubtful stare. "Mid-terms are two weeks away. Relax."

"This is my senior year and I have to stay focused."

She lowered the camera. "It's my senior year too. And I say we should make the most of it."

"You said that last year," I said, placing my hands on my hips. Delaney never took anything seriously, including her schoolwork. Luckily for her, she was naturally smart and a gifted photographer. I knew she had a bright future ahead of her.

Her eyes darted to the side, making sure the mothers weren't listening. "That's because I can never get you to do anything fun. All you do is study and play the piano. But this," she pointed at me, circling her finger, "is all about you. Not me. You're getting married." She chucked my arm and I rolled my eyes at her.

"You're supposed to be in love and excited. Screw exams and thinking about school."

Delaney was right. I should have been in la la land, dreaming about marrying my prince charming. But I just didn't feel it. Something was seriously wrong.

"Easy for you to say. I don't ace exams like you."

"Oh, whatever." She spun around like a hopeless romantic, grabbing a veil from a nearby rack and flinging it over my head. "Bend over so I can fix it." Robotically, my body leaned forward, allowing her to adjust the sheer material over my face. "Okay, take a look."

I took a long hard stare in the mirror as the clicks reverberated in my ear. For the past twenty years, I had been shielded and protected by my parents. I was homeschooled and forced to commute to the university my freshman and sophomore year. College should have marked the time of my life, but it didn't. The veil I wore was so much like the shield I had been wrapped in my entire life. I was ready to tear it down, show the world who I really was, and see what it had to offer.

"No. I don't like it." I yanked the veil out of my hair and tossed it to her.

"Oh, okay." She leaped forward, barely catching it by the end of the material. "We can find another one—"

"Nope. I'm not wearing a veil."

Mom quickly turned in my direction. "What's wrong, sweetie?"

I walked to a counter and picked up a clip decorated in sparkling jewels. "Nothing, I just don't want to wear a veil."

"No veil?" Suzanne asked, a light frown emerging from her porcelain smooth skin.

"Sorry, I don't like the feeling of something hanging in front of my face." Using a vanity mirror, I pulled my hair back and positioned the comb to the side, allowing my brown hair to cascade forward. I smiled, liking the style much more, but the expression of happiness wasn't real. It was forced and had fake written all over it. However, no one seemed to notice because this was the Lexi everyone knew. Sweet, agreeable, quiet, and well respected. Deep down that just wasn't me.

"Well, I suppose," Mom said, with a tone that spelled disappointment.

"Ooo, I like that." Delaney captured another shot while I held the deceptive smile. "I can't wait for June. It's going to be one hell of a party."

With that comment, Suzanne cast a disapproving look at my crazy roommate. Delaney covered her mouth. "Oops, sorry about that."

Delaney didn't always think before she acted. Instead, she made decisions based on impulse and sometimes regretted them. However, that was who she was and she was the one person I knew that really enjoyed life.

"I think the comb is very becoming of you, especially if you wear your hair down." Suzanne placed locks of my hair in front of my chest, trying to cover up my breasts.

Despite all the lace, they were more noticeable and for once, I didn't mind. After all, Mom had convinced me to keep them tucked away and hidden because no respectable girl flaunted her breasts for people to see, especially to guys. Her voice echoed in my head, *only your husband should have the honor of enjoying them at the appropriate time.* If only I could get Collin to enjoy them now before they sagged to my waist.

I eased the comb from my hair and handed it to Suzanne. "I do like it."

"I think we should buy it then," she said, with a gentle smile.

"Mom?"

"I guess," she sighed.

"Thanks. I'll change so we can go."

Dying to get out of that awful dress, I grabbed Delaney's hand and pulled her into the dressing room with me. "Unzip me, please." I held up my hair, waiting to be released from the chastity gown.

"Damn, this zipper's stuck." She tugged on it and my body broke out in a sweat.

"Please don't tell me that," I sighed.

With another tug, she unzipped the constricting bodice. "There we go."

My lungs took in a full breath of air. "Thank God!"

She helped me step out of the heavy dress and I automatically felt twenty pounds lighter. I slipped on my jeans and shirt and stuffed my feet into my Toms.

"Lexi, I'll tell the sales lady we'll take the dress," Mom's voice carried over the dressing room door.

Covering my face with my hands, I shook my head.

"Tell her you don't like it," Delaney whispered in my ear.

My shoulders dropped. "It's pointless." No matter what I wanted, my mother would never agree. I was the result of helicopter parents doused with a thick layer of strict upbringing. My parents feared that I would make the wrong choices and end up pregnant like my mom did in high school with my sister. They did everything in their power to make sure the three of us didn't embarrass or shame the family. At the rate Collin and I were going, they had nothing to worry about.

To make matters worse, my sister set the bar so high that even with high heels on I doubted I could reach it. She was a successful attorney with two children and a partnering husband who worked alongside her battling court cases. They were a match made for high society, fitting in perfectly with the yuppies in upper Dallas with all the money they rolled in and flaunted.

Thank God, I didn't care to wear those high-heels. I was happy working on my degree to be an English teacher. Money didn't matter to me. In the end, all I really wanted was to help kids succeed. More than that, I wanted to be happy and in love. I hoped that by marrying Collin, he would show me love and give me that fairytale ending that I read in romance books; ones that my mother forbade me to have.

I opened the door and walked past my mom and the sales lady. Delaney followed me, staying close behind.

"Lexi, you could have hung the dress on the hanger," Mom scolded as she scampered into the dressing room. "I'm so sorry. She's probably tired. It's been a long day of...trying on dresses."

The sales lady flashed a sardonic smile and said, "We can put the dress on hold for a week, if you are unsure."

"That would be great," I quickly announced.

Mom shook her head. "I'm sure that's the perfect dress for her, she's tried on so many."

"It's the prettiest one by far," Suzanne added.

Delaney turned around to face me and stuck her finger down her throat.

I raised my brows, agreeing. Picking up the skirt of the dress, I gave it one more look over. Before I could answer, my mom spoke up.

"If you can hold the dress, that would be wonderful."

I breathed another sigh of relief. Maybe I wouldn't look like a mid-century prude after all. "Thank you, Mom."

A breeze swept through my hair, kicking up leaves as signs of autumn appeared across the campus. I untied the hoodie from my waist and put it on. In Texas, autumn never lasted more than a few weeks and since Mother Nature was bipolar, you had no idea if it would be a beautiful sunny day or downright frigid. Checking the weather app on my phone had become a daily ritual.

I crossed the street and opened the door to the quaint burger joint where we ate frequently. The smell of the sizzling grill hit me and my stomach growled. Memorabilia from Park Hill

University's various sports teams hung from the walls, showing off their wins over the last decade. To the right, I spied Delaney sitting next to my brother, Luke, in a booth. They appeared to be in a deep conversation. I couldn't help but notice the steady gaze they held on one another.

"Hi." I dropped my backpack on the bench across from them, disrupting their chat.

"Hey, Sis." Luke turned slowly, as if he didn't want to break eye contact.

"I was beginning to wonder if you were coming." Delaney glanced at her phone. "You sent a text about twenty minutes ago."

Uh huh. Are you sure you wanted me to show up?

For the constant denial of having an interest in each other, claiming they had a friend's only status, they were sitting really close to each other. "Sorry, I had to call the writing center. They want me to tutor someone and we were trying to coordinate schedules." I pulled out my wallet. "Did you two already order?"

"Yeah, about five minutes ago." Luke rubbed his chin and I immediately knew something was up. That something had Delaney's name written all over it. Being that he was my twin, I could sense things about him. It was weird, but we had similar quirks, no matter how much we didn't like admitting them.

"I need to hurry. I have to meet a student in forty-five minutes." When I turned around, I stumbled into Collin.

"Lexi." He caught me between his strong arms and I took advantage of the proximity of our bodies.

"Sorry, I didn't see you." I placed my hand on his chest and stared into his pale green eyes, dying to make that connection with him. "Aren't you supposed to be in class?"

He released my arms and unhooked his backpack, placing it on the floor next to the booth.

So much for that wish.

"Professor cancelled it. I sent you a text but when you didn't respond, I figured you might be here. Thought I'd eat lunch with you."

"Great." I smiled, glad that he wanted to spend time with me. Between school and his baseball practices and games, I jumped at any opportunity for us to be together. "Unfortunately, I have to be at work in forty-five minutes."

"That's fine." He shrugged, showing a little too much indifference. "What do you want to eat?"

Collin usually ordered for me and took it upon himself to do things without asking. At first, I liked it, but since the engagement, I seemed like it was more about control than consideration. I was conflicted between longing for discretion and wanting to be closer to him. "Sure. I'll have the chicken and roasted green Chile burger, no fries, and water with lemon."

"Okay. I'll be right back."

I slid into the booth, thinking of the millions of things I had to do and why I agreed to take on another student when I already had two others I was tutoring. I had been working as a student consultant in the writing center since the beginning of my junior year. It was a great way to earn money for expenses and since English was my major, it helped reinforce everything I had learned. I inhaled a deep breath and reminded myself how much I loved helping people and that it would be worth my time.

"You okay, Sis?" Luke placed his hand on mine.

"Yeah, just a lot going on."

"She's stressing about the wedding," Delaney chimed in.

"And school." I plucked out a few napkins from the holder as I tried not to think about my upcoming nuptials.

Luke raised a brow. "The ceremony is in June. Of next year. Isn't it a little early to be worrying?"

I laid the napkins on the table and folded them neatly. "Yes, but there's so much to do and—"

"I get it." Luke held up his hands. "Please, spare me the details."

Collin sat our drinks on the table and then turned to Luke. "Is she obsessing about the wedding again?"

"What do you think?" Luke smirked.

"I told her not to worry about anything. We have plenty of time to get things in order. Delaney you'll be helping as well as the wedding planner, right?" Collin asked.

"Yes, and I told her this should be fun. But you know Lexi—"

"She wants everything to be perfect," Luke added.

"No, I don't." I pounded my fist on the table. "And will you stop talking like I'm not here?"

"I'm sorry." Collin planted a kiss on my cheek. "I didn't mean to be rude. I was only trying to be supportive."

Collin had a funny way of showing his support. And, although I did like things in order, it was mainly because I worked hard to make my parents happy. I saw myself falling into the same trap with Collin and I didn't want to.

"I know. Forget about it," I said as I touched his hand. The bend in his arm caused a bulge to raise under his sleeves. I focused in on the size of his bicep, running my fingers along the ripples and curves.

"Lexi, stop." He brushed my hand off in obvious discomfort.

The waitress arrived with our food and I took my plate and scooted as close to the wall as possible.

Why didn't he want me to touch him? I couldn't understand it. As much as I didn't want to think about it, I couldn't stop obsessing over it. Maybe it was because I knew I was making the wrong decision.

Or was I?

Even though we had agreed to wait until marriage to have sex, I longed for him to hold me and caress me. Instead, he pushed me away. Time after time, he snubbed what little romance we had between us. I needed to feel that soulful connection. I had to know that we were making the right decision and that we were more than just friends. I was dying for more than his sweet terms of endearment.

"Are you headed to the gym later on?" my brother asked Collin.

"Of course," Collin replied, waiting to take a bite of his burger. "I can't slow down even if it's the off season."

"Me either. Spring training kicked my butt last year. And coach will be..."

I zoned out as they continued talking about baseball. Luke and Collin had played ball together through a homeschool athletic association during their high school years. That was how we met. Coincidentally, they were recruited to play for Park Hill University and my parents gave me no other option for my education.

"Lexi?" Delaney waved a hand in front of my face.

"Huh?" I stopped chewing for a second.

She shook her head and I knew she thought I was thinking about how perfect I wanted my wedding. I needed to confide in her and then man up and have a serious 'come to Jesus' talk with Collin. My head was a convoluted mess of wants, needs, rules, and fears that was sending me quickly to the edge of insanity.

"So, do you want to or not?"

I swallowed my food, realizing I hadn't listened to a word she had said. "Do what?"

"Seriously?" Delaney placed a hand on her forehead. "You didn't hear me?"

"Sorry," I mouthed.

"I asked if you wanted to go to the gym with me."

"You know I don't like to work out." I took another bite of my burger.

"I know, but I thought you'd like to tone up your arms," she flexed her bicep, "since you're thinking about buying that strapless wedding dress."

I kicked her under the table.

"Ow!"

I didn't want Collin to know what type of dress I'd be wearing and now Delaney had ruined it.

"You bought a strapless dress?" Collin immediately keyed in on our conversation. I smiled, glad that it sprung a reaction from him, regardless of whether it was good or bad.

"Well, I haven't bought it yet." Knowing my mom, she wouldn't allow me to buy it either, but I had to at least push for it.

"Sorry." Delaney squeezed her eyes shut for a brief moment. "I just didn't want to go alone." A spark flickered in her light blue eyes and it became clear to me that she wanted to go because of my brother.

"Oh, all right. But you and I are going to have a talk." I pointed my finger at her. She retreated in her chair, knowing I was peeved. Checking my phone, I saw that I had twenty minutes until my meeting. "I gotta go."

"But you didn't finish your burger." Collin glanced at my half-eaten plate of food.

"I guess I wasn't that hungry." I stuffed my phone in the outside pocket of my backpack.

"I'll call you later." Collin placed a hand on my arm and leaned forward.

"Okay." I aligned my head so that my lips targeted his. I closed my eyes in anticipation of his kiss and held my breath to restrain the butterflies threatening to take flight from the pit of my stomach. Instead, Collin's lips landed on my forehead. I could only imagine how silly I looked with my eyes closed and lips puckered.

Why wouldn't he kiss me on the lips?

"You'd better go." He rubbed my arm, giving me a nice warm up as if I were cold. "You don't want to be late."

I hitched my backpack over my shoulder and my body caved in from the weight. "See y'all later." I scooted out of the booth and shuffled through the door. As I headed to the campus, I told myself not to give much thought to what happened. Who was I kidding? Did Collin really want to marry me? He sure didn't act like it. Then again, neither did I.

Σ

Chapter 2

"Hi, Lexi." Sara adjusted her red glasses as I entered the small office located in Ramsey Hall. She was sitting at one of the computers typing in some information as one of the students she tutored gathered their books.

"Hey, Sara." I waved back.

The more I thought about it, the more I really didn't feel like meeting with this guy. My personal life was more than I could handle and I doubted my ability to give him one-hundred percent of my attention.

The door to Dr. Raymond Phillips', director for the writing center, office opened. "Lexi," he pointed at me, "I need to see you in my office before your appointment."

Dr. Phillips tended to be high-strung and a little ADD. He functioned like an Energizer bunny on nuclear power, zipping around the office and saying random comments left and right. Just watching him made me tired. Aside from his madness, he was a wonderful boss and mentor. I really enjoyed working for him regardless of the fact that I needed to wear inline skates just to keep up with him.

"Yes, sir."

As I passed Kyler, a graduate student and a gifted writer with two non-fiction books published on the wars of Texas, he raised a brow. He didn't have to say anything because I knew what he was thinking. Better you than me.

"Sit, please." Dr. Phillips shuffled a stack of papers on his desk and fumbled with a few other things. He seemed awkwardly quiet.

I shut the door behind me. "Is everything okay?"

"Yes," he nodded, though the expression on his face was less than convincing. "I thought it might be wise to enlighten you about the student you will be working with."

"Sara gave me the details, I think I'm good," I offered as I sat in the chair in front of his desk.

He smirked. "Well, I don't see how that is possible being that I just got off the phone with Coach Anderson."

"The football coach?" My stomach tensed and I was suddenly glad I didn't finish my lunch. I had heard a few stories about football players who had made their way into college but lacked the ability to write. If professors wouldn't pass them, they usually ended up in the writing center, relying on tutors to help them learn.

He perched on the edge of his chair, still fumbling through his paperwork. "Yes, the one and only."

I hesitated, but asked, "Well, what did he say?"

"Ah ha, here it is." Dr. Phillips wiggled a cream folder from under the mountain-high stack of papers. He opened the folder and his eyes quickly scanned the pages. I heard his leg rock underneath the desk and it made my stomach clench tighter. "I need you to give this student one-hundred percent of your best ability. I can reassign the other two students you have been working with if you are unable to handle the load."

Great.

"Why me?" I placed a hand over my chest. "I mean, maybe it's best if he works with a graduate student or one of the other professors in the center. I'm not that qualified."

"Stop discounting your abilities. You are one of the best undergraduate consultants I have working in the center, and frankly, I don't know whom else to pair this student with."

I leaned back against the chair, feeling the pressure build in my chest. "Thanks for the compliment, but this sounds crucial, especially if the coach called you."

He pressed his lips together and let out an audible breath. "It is and I am going to be honest with you. I've already had him work with two others and it didn't work out. So, I'm counting on you to help him. Or, I should say, Coach Anderson is counting on you."

Swallowing the lump that had quickly formed in the back of my throat, I managed to say, "He is?"

"And so are the fans, alumni, students..."

A good reason why I shouldn't agree to help this guy.

"What exactly do I need to do? I mean, what does he need help with?"

Dr. Phillips handed me the folder. "Here are copies of his papers and reports that Dr. Connor and Lisa Jenkins advised him on. I suggest you review them before he arrives." He glanced at his watch. "Which doesn't afford you much time."

I quickly scanned through the papers, taking note of the red marks and sideline comments. "From what I can tell, he's in serious need of a lesson in grammar 101."

"Exactly." A smile formed across the director's face. "According to Dr. Connor and Lisa, they worked with him on structure, outline, and formation, but he also needs some help with common punctuation and grammatical errors."

"Why didn't they help him with that?"

"Lisa intended to, but their personalities clashed so she refused to work with him further."

A laugh escaped. "And that's our problem?"

The professor winced. "Lexi, I'm surprised you don't want to help."

Meet the new Lexi Thompson.

I shrugged. "Sorry, I just don't see how this is fair."

This was exactly what I thought it was — another jock that had paid someone to write his entrance essay. His momma and daddy, who were probably alumni, had more than likely bribed someone of influence so their star-athlete son could play. I loved helping people but not those who cheated their way into school. Helping him was the last thing I wanted to do. This was college, not high school. I didn't care if he flunked out or got kicked off the team.

"I know. It shouldn't be, but unfortunately, Coach Anderson has asked us to help him. Or rather, has said he expects us to help him."

What? I didn't sign up for this.

"I can't make him learn or pass his classes." I shut the folder. I didn't have to read any more notes. His type was clear to me. "What makes you think we can work together?"

The director paused, which was rare, and I could tell he was deciding what information to share with me. There was definitely more to this story. "You have a lot of patience and you're friendly. Not to mention, I think you're a damn good teacher. I'm positive he will connect with you and take kindly to your assistance."

"Oh, great." I threw my hands up in the air. "He doesn't even want to admit he needs help."

Crossing his arms, the director raised a brow. "I didn't say that. He is here on his own accord. The coach has high hopes for him and knows he can get his act together and succeed. He needs a strong tutor and lots of encouragement. PHU also has him in a program and... well, I'll leave it at that."

A sour taste formed in the back of my mouth. I knew exactly who this was without even looking at the name on the edge of the file folder.

Raven Davenport.

I stepped out of the director's office, entered the main area, and there, standing in all of his six-foot-two glory, was the star quarterback for PHU's football team. I had never seen him in person and I felt so small looking up at him. Even though I didn't know him personally, I'd heard and read enough about him to know he was a womanizer with a drug problem.

Another reason why I shouldn't help him.

"Hi, I'm Lexi Thompson and I've been asked to consult with you." I made it clear that it wasn't my choice to help him.

"Lexi. Hmm, I like that name."

Uh, no you don't.

His full lips spread, revealing the most charming smile, coupled with a deep dimple on the right. Now I knew why every girl fell for him. I, however, was smarter than that. "I'm Raven." He stalled for a moment, his eyes giving me a thorough exam to the point that I bet he knew what color my panties were. "Raven Davenport." He ran a hand over his short buzz cut and looked like the perfect model for an Abercrombie and Fitch ad.

He was toxic and smelled of sex and drugs. Well, not that I knew what all that smelled like, but his aura beamed bright red, warning me to be careful.

"Are you ready to get started? We only have an hour." I held out my hand, motioning to a small table in the corner.

"That's plenty of time." He raised his brows.

I rolled my eyes and walked to the table. Taking a seat, I took out the agreement that Dr. Phillips had prepared. I signed my name and moved the papers in front of him. "Please sign this."

Raven leaned over the table. "I was thinking you might want to do this somewhere more private." A seductive grin spread across his lips as he pressed his weight against the table, as if testing the durability of the wood.

My jaw dropped. Was he serious? My fiancé didn't even tease me that way. Although, that would've been nice. Then again, we hadn't even made out on a bed much less on a table. I had to restrain myself from slapping him.

"Excuse me, Mr. Davenport?"

He pulled out a chair and sat down. "You can call me Raven." I guess by the tone in my voice, he knew I meant business.

"Please read the agreement and let me know if you have any questions. I indicated that we would meet twice a week for an hour, and more if a mutual agreement can be established."

"Okay. Sounds fair. Do you have a pen?" He held out his hand, his long fingers curled up in a perfect cup. A hand that was made for a football and caressing various female parts.

Whoa! Where did that come from?

Extending my hand, I gave him my pen. He eased it from my fingertips in a gentle motion. "Thank you, Lexi."

He signed the paper and handed it back to me.

"Aren't you going to read it?"

Shaking his head, he said, "No, I trust you."

"You don't even know me."

"Not yet." His green eyes sparkled. "But my gut tells me we're going to get to know each other real well."

It was obvious why Lisa didn't want to work with him. I made a mental note to call her the second he left. I sucked in a quick breath and let it out to clear my head. "Whatever." Hastily, I removed my Hodge's Harbrace Handbook and another pen from my backpack. I opened the folder Dr. Phillips had given me and took out his papers.

"I reviewed your file and—"

"You and everybody else." His head lowered and his shoulders sank.

I continued, unsure of how to handle his comment. "I have an idea of where you need the most help with your writing."

His head popped up and a layer of relief removed the downward slope of his lips. "You do?"

"Yes. I think we should start with some grammar basics." I opened the book to the first chapter and moved it between us. I placed one of his papers below the book, preparing to show him examples so he could relate easily to the concepts. "First, I'll give you a quick and dirty overview of the parts of speech."

He moved his chair closer to me and the scent of fresh juniper and bergamot swept over me. The guy smelled like a cologne insert from one of my magazines. I tried not to breathe it in, but the harder I tried, the more I realized I loved the smell.

Darn, I wish Collin smelled this good.

He flashed me a grin. "I like it quick and dirty."

I wanted to slap myself. Could I have chosen a worse thing to say? "I'm sure you do, Raven. I mean, you're a guy and a football player."

"True," a half smile formed, "but not every guy likes to do things quickly or get messy while doing them."

A rush of heat inundated me. I yanked a hair band off my wrist and pulled my hair up in a messy bun. I raised the sleeves on my shirt and braced myself.

I'll be damned if I let this jerk get to me.

Ignoring his comment, I pressed forward with my instruction. Raven listened intently and nodded his head while asking relative questions. When the guy wasn't being a huge flirt, he was actually pleasant to be around. I felt sorry for him because he had gone through school without learning proper grammar rules. No wonder he couldn't write a proper sentence. Oddly enough, his verbal skills seemed fine; his written skills, on the other hand... well, that was another story.

Helping him might not be so bad after all.

After forty minutes of reviewing grammar syntax, he began to lose interest. He shifted his weight and yawned a few times, stretching his arms. I scooted to the edge of my chair, praying he wouldn't rest his elbow behind me. Before he lowered his arms, his phone buzzed. His eyes widened with delight as he looked at the screen.

"Excuse me. I need to take this call."

"Um, no, you can't." I pointed to a sign on the wall. "Policy says—"

"Hey, baby, what's up?" He answered the phone, ignoring me.

He rambled on about his schedule and practice for a minute or so before shifting gears. I contemplated getting up to tell Dr. Phillips. That would mean instant removal from the writing center and I wouldn't have to help him. Then again, it probably wouldn't matter because the coach had called in a favor. I started to stand but stopped when the lure of his voice made it too hard to resist listening to his conversation. His smitten words rolled off his tongue and he sounded like Eros himself. Warmth rose from my belly and I turned around to see who else was in the center. Luckily, Sara had already left and Kyler was talking to a student, not paying any attention.

Raven was having phone sex. Right there in front of me, in the writing center of all places.

Visions flashed through my mind and my face burned. I covered my ears, trying to block out his words, but it didn't help. My heart raced and my breath quickened. I shifted in my chair, crossing my legs tightly until my feet went numb.

"Yeah, baby, right there." He winked at me.

I gasped. "I'll be right back." I rushed out of the room and headed straight for the bathroom.

Closing the door to the lounge located next to the stalls, I paced the small room as I fanned myself. Being a virgin, I had never come close to experiencing anything so dirty yet sensual at the same time. And, the worst part, it wasn't even directed at me! The guy was blessed with sexual creativity. Why the heck didn't he gear some of that imagination toward his schoolwork?

Sure, I had read those types of sex scenes in romance books, but it was entirely different hearing them firsthand. Well, secondhand in that case. Nonetheless, I had just become hyperaware of tingles and sensations caused by an actual human being.

A guy that was sitting next me, not even touching me.

And the saddest part of it all? That guy wasn't Collin.

I sighed as I collapsed onto the cushioned bench. The situation wasn't good and every warning light was flashing.

Reason number three: don't lust over something that isn't yours.

Σ

Chapter 3

I crashed on my bed, drained from the tutoring session with Raven. The guy was the epitome of a bad boy filled with lust, temptation, and sin that women dreamed of experiencing.

Including me.

He had opened my eyes and I knew exactly what I was missing in my relationship with Collin.

Passion.

Intimacy.

Not to mention, sex.

I had to stop pretending that everything was all right between us because it wasn't. If we were in love, we sure didn't act like it. Something was wrong with this picture, but I wasn't giving up yet. I really did care for Collin. He was a wonderful guy that respected me, honored me, and would never do me wrong. I had to demonstrate the emotions flowing within me in hopes that he would respond willingly to my plea for his affection. I owed this to myself — to us.

Burying my head in my pillow, I prayed for strength.

"Lexi, wake up." A nudge woke me from a deep sleep.

"W-what?" I pulled the covers over my head. "Leave me alone."

"You promised to go to the gym with me," Delaney pleaded, yanking the blankets off me. A chill spread over my body and I reached for the fleece. "C'mon, Lex."

When she shortened my name, I knew she was serious. Giving in, I rolled out of bed. "Okay. I'm up."

As I changed my clothes, I watched Delaney carefully. She looked way too excited to go sweat and torture herself with weights and medicine balls. Although I didn't care if she and my brother hooked up, I wanted to know the truth. If I asked my brother, I doubt he'd tell me anything. Even though we were close growing up, we had distanced ourselves since being in college. He never shared his thoughts or feelings about girls, and vice versa. He kept it all to himself and I couldn't help but wonder if it was due to our parent's strict upbringing or if he was just as inexperienced as I was. Regardless, I'd make one of them spill it.

Delaney reached for the doorknob and I stuck out my hand, stopping her from opening it. "Before we go, I need to ask you something."

"What?" Her eyes bulged and her chest rose rapidly. "What is it?"

"What's up between you and Luke?"

"Your brother?"

I crossed my arms and narrowed my eyes at her. "Yes, my brother."

"N-nothing. Why?" She pulled the rubber band out of her long, dark hair and moved toward the mirror to redo her ponytail. Her hands worked quickly and she fidgeted, becoming more frustrated with her strands of tangled hair.

"Don't lie to me, Laney."

She flung around, knowing that when I used her nickname, I meant business, too.

"Why do you think something's up between us?" She approached me head-on and I noticed that she had on too much makeup for working out. Her lips were a perfect shiny nude and her cheeks had a shimmering rose tint, not to mention the thick layer of eyeliner coupled with lashes maxed out in mascara.

"Because of the way you two have been acting around each other."

"And how's that? We're not acting differently."

"Seriously?" I laughed. Delaney couldn't hold a poker face to save her life. Then again, neither could I. That's why I knew I could trust her. She was a genuine, no nonsense kind of girl. An only child brought up on a farm with goats and chickens by her adopted parents, she was the wild, country girl that had basically seen and done everything before arriving at college. Despite her cute Texas twang, she warned me that she wasn't innocent and knew how to party with the big boys.

"You two have been talking a lot when I'm not around."

"I'm sorry," she said, adjusting her workout-top that made her boobs pop out. "I won't talk to him again if it bothers you that much."

"I didn't say that." Relaxing my shoulders, I placed my hand on her arm. "If you want to date him, I'm okay with that; I'd just like to know."

She let out a deep breath. "Well, we're not dating, so you don't have anything to worry about." Giving a quick glance to her phone, she said, "Let's go. I want to try out this new class called Yogalates. You should try it with me."

"No thanks. I'm going to work out with Collin."

"Oh." She winked as we headed to the rec center.

If I could only be so lucky.

We entered the gym and spotted Collin and Luke at the free weights along with several other guys testing their manhood as they grunted and moaned while pressing the weights. I had to admit, the scene was divine, but I zeroed in on my guy. A thin sheen of sweat covered his face and arms and I couldn't help but imagine how he would look naked, hovering over my body after a round of hot sex.

Oh my God! Why is that the first thing that pops into my head?

No matter how hard I tried to keep my mind from going there, I couldn't deny what I wanted and needed from him. My body was crying out for his attention.

"I'll meet you in an hour," Delaney informed me as she went in the opposite direction.

"Okay, see you later."

I approached Collin from behind and turned on my sexy voice. "Are you working out hard?"

He flinched and nearly dropped the weight. "Lexi," he said with an exacerbated breath, "I didn't hear you behind me."

"Sorry." I fingered his sandy blond hair, eager to dive my hands through his thick layers. He tilted his head away from my hand and I got the message. He didn't want me to touch him. But I wasn't giving up.

"Don't ever do that." He wiped his face with his hand towel. "I could have hurt myself or worse, hurt you."

"Whatever." I waved off his exaggerated remark, although it hurt because I wanted him to respond willingly to my teasing. "I thought you could work me out. You know, show me your routine." I leaned against the arm curl bench, trying to entice him.

"You want me to show you how to work out?" He shifted the dumbbell to his other hand, his eyes darting back and forth between me and the mirror in front of him.

"Yes, please." I bit down on my lower lip, trying to pull off an erotic look.

"Why don't you ask your brother? He's the trainer."

"If you want, I can show you a few things," Luke puffed before pressing a bar up in the air.

Luke was majoring in Exercise Sport Science and worked part-time at the rec center. If he didn't land a contract with a professional baseball team, his backup plan was to be a trainer. We both knew he was only playing to appease my parents. In reality, he would be the best one to train me, but I didn't want that.

"I was hoping to spend some time with you." I dragged two fingers along the curves of muscles in his forearm, leaving behind a trail of bumps.

Collin dropped the weight with a loud thud. "Um... we can start with the machines." He got up from the bench, adjusting his shorts, and then picked up the dumbbell.

Yes!

"Hey, Sis, did you come by yourself?" Luke took a few deep breaths as he moved his head from side to side, popping his bones.

"Stop. I hate when you do that." I shuddered, trying to displace the visual. I don't know why the sound gave me the hebegeebees, but it did. "No, I came with Delaney."

"Oh, you did?" He looked around, expressing a little too much interest in locating her.

"Yeah, she's in some yoga class."

"Okay. I'll find her later." He sat down on a bench and resumed his workout.

I eyed him for a moment, debating if I should ask him what was going on between them, but I was too anxious to work out with Collin.

"I'm going to show her a few things and then I'll be back," Collin informed Luke while nodding at me to follow him.

"Later," Luke responded.

I latched on to his arm as he led the way to a row of machine weights. He leaned over and I watched him closely as he adjusted the weight and sat down. "So, what you are going to do is bring your arms together in a slow, controlled movement. Like this," he said, demonstrating the movement. I watched the muscles swell from under his shirt. With each squeeze, they tensed and it teased me. I told myself to take things slow, but my body was humming with desire. I was dying to touch him, feel him, run my hands all over his body.

Something I had never done before.

Something I wanted to do.

"Then, release it back into position slowly." He smiled at me with soft, pillowy lips.

"Okay," I responded, though I wasn't paying much attention. My head spun as a beckoning call simmered inside of me, urging me to take action. Grabbing his face between my hands, I pressed my lips to his. I thrust my tongue into his mouth, eager to taste him, and released all of the endorphins that had built up over time.

In one swift movement, he pushed me away. "Lexi, what are you doing?" He wiped his lips with the back of his hand, removing my taste from him, as though he didn't want any trace of me on him.

My heart sank.

Why didn't he want me?

"Sorry, I just... I couldn't resist you." I bit back the tears, refusing to cry. Maybe that was what I needed to do. Cry and beg him to take me. Prove that we weren't making the wrong decision.

Was it a crime for our tongues to cross? Did he not find me attractive?

I noticed the other girls in the gym. My lanky body couldn't compete with their curvy legs and perfect bubble butts. Dressed in their skin-tight yoga pants and push-up exercise bras, I looked like a homeless person in baggy sweats and a worn out PHU T-shirt. No wonder he didn't want me. I was nothing compared to these girls. Instead of crying and begging for his forgiveness, I let the wrong emotion take over.

Anger.

"You need to control yourself. We are in public." He looked around, ensuring no one was paying attention to us.

"Let them watch," I said boldly, testing my limits. "You're my fiancé. If I want to kiss you, I will." I had been patient, respecting his wishes of waiting to have sex until marriage. The least he could do was express how he felt about me, show me how much he loved me.

I needed him to caress me.

Kiss me.

Tease me.

Hell, at least flirt with me.

Do something aside from being kind and respectful. I was tired of waiting for him to take the reins. Unfortunately, my decision to take control failed. I had been deprived my entire life. I had been a good girl for way too long, always doing what my parents asked of me.

Perfect, respectful, honorable Lexi.

I may have landed a damn hot guy, but what did it matter if he resisted showing me his love?

He ran a hand down his face. "We need to be more respectful—"

"It was just a kiss," I interrupted, crossing my arms and balling my hands tightly underneath me. I felt the need to defend my actions. To my fiancé. The man I was supposed to marry. The man who was supposed to be my happily ever after.

He tilted his head to the side. His boyish charm made it difficult to stay mad, but I held my ground.

"You were sticking your tongue down my throat."

"And?" I bit back the string of expletive words dying to come out of my mouth.

"That's not being discrete and it sure isn't honoring you."

"Oh, to hell with my honor! I want you to just—"

"Lexi, what's wrong with you?" He stood up and crossed his arms, as if ready to challenge me. "You're acting crazy."

"No, I'm not." I stomped my foot.

"Yes, you are," he sneered.

I knew I was acting childish and Collin pointing it out only made it worse. "Forget it." I threw my hands up in the air.

"You're so damn reserved at times... it drives me crazy." I spun on my heels and headed for the door.

"Lexi, wait," he called, but I picked up the pace until I was running. Even though I knew that was the wrong thing to do, I didn't know how to handle the rejection. I was such a failure. Love really sucked. I thought I could entice Collin. Instead, I only pushed him away.

Hot tears streamed down my face as I ran to Charter Hall. I resisted the urge to turn around to see if Collin was following me, but I had a feeling I was alone. As I ran up the steps, I wiped away the evidence of my pain. After all, I was being stupid. Collin did love me. When it came to expressing his feelings, he just didn't know how. He was so hung up on honoring me that he failed to realize how much I needed his affection.

He had to care about me, right?

Otherwise, why had he asked me to marry him? Confusion clouded my brain and there was only one thing I knew would help.

I passed through the foyer of my dormitory and entered the lounge area. Easing onto the padded bench, I placed my hands on the ivory keys of the large grand piano. I had been playing since I was a child and used it to de-stress on a regular basis. The beautiful sound always relaxed me and I found myself playing for hours at a time. My fingers strummed across the bars, choosing to play, *Say Something,* a song Delaney had begged me to learn. I had told her it was the most depressing song ever, but it fit my situation perfectly. Recalling the words, I whispered them under my breath.

The tears reappeared, but I didn't bother to wipe them away. Big drops fell as I pounded the keyboard, pouring my heart and soul into it. Why was life so painful? Getting married was supposed to be a joyous occasion, not heart wrenching. All the signs were there, I was just avoiding them at all costs.

If Collin would only love me the way I deserved to be loved.

"Lexi?" Delaney placed a hand on my shoulder. "Are you okay?"

I stopped playing. Unable to look at her, I buried my face in my hands and wept uncontrollably. She wrapped her arms around me and hugged me tightly.

"What happened? Collin said you got mad and left."

"I can't do this, Delaney," I mumbled through sobbing gasps.

"Do what? What are you talking about?" She handed me a couple of tissues and I wiped my eyes and nose.

I tried to talk, but the tears wouldn't stop. Every emotion, every doubt, washed down my cheeks in an uncontrollable stream.

"Come on. Let's go."

She wrapped her arm around my shoulders and led me upstairs to the suite we shared. She sat me on my bed and handed me a bottle of water. I took a few sips, but it didn't help. I couldn't breathe, couldn't gain control. These emotions had been tearing me apart on the inside and I had held them back for too long. They wouldn't be trapped any longer. Pulling my hair to the side, she placed a cool washcloth on the back of my neck.

"Look at me, Lexi."

I peeked from behind the wad of tissues.

"I want you to relax and take a few deep breaths." She mimicked the action, extending her hands out to the side. I couldn't help laughing. She must have learned it from her yoga class.

Laughing and crying, I was one hot mess.

"What? What's so funny?" Confusion tainted her question.

Shaking my head, I leaned against her. "Things are so screwed up between Collin and me."

She embraced my cheek with her right hand. "Do you want to talk about it?"

Even though we were friends, I had never shared details about our relationship, aside from telling her how wonderful he was and how lucky I was to have him. The more I thought about it, the more I realized that Collin and I were friends, nothing more. Not even friends with benefits.

"Collin refuses to show me any affection."

With a raised brow, she said, "I've noticed he's not the affectionate type."

"And it sucks because he won't have sex with me," I mumbled.

Her head jerked. "What do you mean? Like tonight or..."

"Ever. Until we're married," I clarified.

She grabbed the water bottle from my hand and took a huge gulp. "You mean to tell me y'all have never done it?"

My head fell to my chest. "Nope. We're virgins."

"Seriously?"

I nodded, embarrassed to admit why I was crying.

She took a deep breath. "I just thought he was the private type. You know, preferring to keep things between you and him. I figured you two were screwing at his place."

"Gross." I cringed and my body shivered. "He lives with my brother and two other guys."

"So." She threw her hands up in the air, like it was no big deal. "He has his own room, doesn't he?"

"Yeah, but my brother would probably tell my parents."

She threw herself back, hitting the bed. "My God, you are a twenty-year-old woman who's engaged to be married. Your parents need to get over this, and so does Luke. This isn't the nineteen-fifties for crying out loud! You two need to test the waters before you say, 'I do'."

"Tell me about it," I sighed.

"And how long have you two been together?"

"Four years."

"Damn, that's a long time to wait." Leaning on her elbows, she said, "Please tell me you two have at least spent the night together somewhere?"

"When was the last time you saw him stay here with me?"

She tapped a finger to her lips. "Uh... come to think of it, never. What about when I'm gone? Speaking of, I'm going to the farm this weekend. It's my dad's birthday, so you'll have the place to yourself."

Another tear escaped. "It won't make a difference if you're gone or not. He refuses to lay next to me, touch me..."

Her mouth fell open for a quick second. "Now that's extreme. What's wrong with that boy?"

I shook my head. "His parents are really hardcore when it comes to their beliefs."

"Their beliefs in what?"

Taking in a deep breath, I explained, "A while back, when I was at their house, I saw this book lying on the kitchen counter. It caught my attention, so I thumbed through it. It was about teaching your kids to not have sex before marriage."

"Okay." She leaned in further, waiting for me to tell her more.

"It also promoted homeschooling, keeping your children safe from the outside world, preparing your daughters to be homemakers, and instilling no dating, no kissing, no touching..."

"What the hell? No one can shelter their kids to that extent, unless they are trying to raise a priest or something."

I stared at the picture of me with my family on my desk. "Well, that's what my parents have tried to do to me and Luke. That's why I'm sick of this. I can't live like this any longer." It was clear why they wanted me to be a teacher. They had my life completely planned for me and I hated them for that.

"Shit. I just thought your parents were really overprotective."

"Yeah, me too. I kind of understand where Collin's coming from when he tells me he has to abide by his father's wishes and remain a virgin until marriage."

"Oh, hell no," she pulled the band out of her hair, "that wouldn't work for me."

I sighed. "I know! It's not working for me either. I need that level of intimacy with him."

"I don't know how you've lasted this long." She worked the tangles out of her hair. "I have to take a test drive. You know... make sure I can shift his gears and ensure he knows how to put the pedal to the metal."

"Laney, TMI!"

"Sorry, but if he can't make me scream, there's no point."

"Lalalala." I placed my hands over my ears. "I can't hear you."

She pulled my hands away. "Stop, you're acting like a child."

"Well, I don't want to know how you like it. It was bad enough that I had to hear you the other night."

"Oh my God, no you didn't." Her face turned beet red.

"Yes, I did."

"But my room's on the other side of the living room," she reasoned, confusion spreading across her face.

"You're quite loud and these walls are paper thin," I reminded her.

"Sorry." Her voice lilted a plea of forgiveness. "Don't take this the wrong way, but what did you expect? Collin's a preacher's son." She quickly averted, focusing on my dilemma.

I lifted my feet to the bed, resting my chin against my knees. "I know, but aren't they supposed to be the worst ones?"

"Well, let me put it this way, the ones I knew back home weren't virgins. I can tell you from first-hand experience."

"Oh, Laney, why couldn't my life have been more like yours?"

She sprung up. "Wait a minute — you have no idea what you're wishing for. My life was far from good."

"Yeah, but it beats being kept under lock and key and deprived of enjoying life."

"Maybe, but..." She popped the band around her wrist a few times. "Never mind. I don't want to talk about my life right now. This is about you." Delaney always avoided sharing details about her childhood. All I knew was that her parents had died when she was young. Her pain and hurt was obvious, even after many years.

I let out another big sigh. "I'm just so confused. I don't know what to do."

She raised a brow. "What's your gut telling you to do?"

"Oh, I don't know." My throat tightened, refusing to speak the truth.

She continued popping the rubber band and even though it agitated me, I figured it was a way for her to self soothe, so I didn't say anything. "Don't stop, keep going. It's good to get this out in the open."

"I-I don't know if I should marry Collin."

"Whoa!" The rubber band snapped in half, flying in two separate directions. "Are you sure about that?"

Thoughts ravaged my mind. I wasn't sure of anything at that point. "I don't know, I just... ugh! I feel like I need something, *anything* to prove to me that he loves me."

"Just because you two haven't had sex doesn't mean he doesn't love you."

"I know that." I roughly wiped another stray tear. "But when I'm with him, I don't feel anything... God, Laney, I feel like we're just friends. Like our relationship is strictly platonic."

"Are you attracted to him?"

"Of course I am. He's good looking and has a damn hot body."

If only I could see him naked.

"And tonight, I actually got brave and tried to come on to him, but he pushed me away."

"Why do you think he did that, aside from not wanting to have sex?"

Delaney always asked the good questions; too bad she never asked herself those questions before doing stuff she later regretted.

"He claimed that French kissing wasn't honoring me and we shouldn't be doing that in public." I heaved a deep breath. "Why won't he make out with me? It's not like the fires of Hell are going to consume him." I threw my hands up in the air as the frustration released. "I'm his finance, damn it! That has to stand for something, right?"

Delaney nodded, allowing me to vent all my frustrations. "It should. Y'all do that stuff in private, right?"

"No," I whined.

"What?" The whites of her eyes bulged. "You're kidding right?"

"I'm telling you, we've only shared sweet kisses and held hands. What if things don't get better once we're married? What am I supposed to do then? Marriage is a huge step and I... I just don't know if I'm ready for that." I squeezed my arms tighter around my body, convincing myself that it was okay to admit the truth.

"Look," she sighed, "I'm going to be honest with you. Regardless of staying on home plate, you should both have a strong attraction toward one another and be in love. Like, visibly in love."

She stared at me, waiting for an answer. I turned my head, averting her questioning gaze.

"You're in love with him, aren't you?"

Nodding, I said, "Well, yeah. I've been with him forever."

"Just because you two have been together for four years doesn't mean you should get married."

"I know, but our parents, family, and friends are expecting us to marry."

"Lexi, that's not why people get married." She latched on to both of my arms, forcing me to look at her. "People agree to marry because they are in love and can't live without each other. Their feelings run deep and in essence have become one. They know that they can't live without the other. Do you and Collin have that type of love?"

I pressed my lips together. "Sweet pecks and holding hands isn't enough for me to know."

"Then you need to ask yourself a very important question."

I hesitated for a moment, searching her eyes for what she was trying to make me see. "Do we love each other enough to get married?"

"Exactly."

Σ

Chapter 4

It took me the rest of the week to pull myself together, but I still wasn't sure how to solve my problem. Collin had texted me that night, apologizing if he hurt my feelings. Eager to move forward, I forgave him and told him I was sorry, too. Thankfully, Raven had canceled our Thursday session so I didn't have him to distract me. As an offering of peace, Collin asked me out on a date and I chose a movie.

I took my time getting dressed, making sure I had the perfect outfit, makeup and hair. My number one goal was to look sexy for Collin. If we were getting married, I had to make sure he was attracted to me. Like Delaney had said, we needed an unfailing love for one another that warranted marriage. Not only did I owe it to myself, but to him. We deserved to be with someone we loved wholeheartedly, not just someone we cared about.

My phone chimed and I eagerly picked it up.

Collin: I'm outside waiting for you.

Me: I'm on my way.

"Delaney, I'm leaving," I yelled from across the suite.

She rushed into my dorm room. "Wow, you look good," she said, giving me a once over.

"I don't look desperate, do I?" I bent down, pushing the socks under my knee-high black boots.

"Well, you are? Aren't you?"

I looked up, shocked at her comment.

A smile formed across her face. "Relax, I'm just kidding. You look cute and sexy."

"Well, I wasn't going for cute, but I'll take sexy."

Rearranging my strands of curls, she said, "If this ensemble doesn't tempt Collin, then I'd have to say that he's gay."

I burst out in laughter. "What?"

She shrugged. "Just saying."

"No, I don't think so. I mean..." I paused for a moment, pondering her comment. What if she was right? Was he marrying me to please his family and hide his sexual preference? "I hope not."

"Me too, because that would be a waste of a good piece of ass."

"Laney!" I slapped her arm. "That's my fiancé you're talking about."

"Sorry."

My phone chimed again. Giving it a quick glance, I said, "I better go. He's waiting for me."

"Have a great time and do everything I would do, okay?" she snickered.

"I'll try." I did one last check in the mirror, grabbed my handbag and sweater, and headed out the door.

I walked through the campus commons and toward the small drive where Collin stood outside his pick-up truck with the door open. A gust of air swept between the buildings, kicking up my short, ruffled mini skirt. My hand automatically went down to stop it, but I let go for a quick second, giving Collin a sneak peak. His eyes widened with delight and then he quickly made eye contact with me.

"Breezy tonight?" His voice trembled and I knew that little unplanned event excited him.

"Sure is." I leaned forward and kissed him on the lips. He responded favorably, puckering his lips against mine.

A shudder trickled up my spine, reassuring me this would be a good night.

On the way to the theater, we engaged in small talk. I wanted to discuss our relationship, but I needed more time than the fifteen-minute drive. Collin displayed his perfect manners, opening the doors for me and even holding my hand as we walked from the parking lot to the theater.

"What movie do you want to see?" Collin glanced at the screens as he removed his wallet from his pocket.

"Mortal Instruments," I said, unable to contain the excitement. The movie had been out for over a month but due to schoolwork, I hadn't had the chance to see it.

His brows knitted and a deep line formed across his forehead. "What's it about?"

"Relax, you'll like it." I rubbed his arm.

He pinned me with a doubtful look. "Is it based on a book?"

"Of course it is," I smiled. "All the good movies are based on books."

"I guess." He nodded with indifference and handed the girl behind the counter his check card.

Entering the auditorium, I quickly took the lead and chose two chairs in the back corner.

"You want to sit this far back?" He scanned the room looking for a closer seat for us.

"Yes, this is fine." I quickly sat down, not giving him the opportunity to move to another aisle. I did want to sit closer, but I hoped that sitting in the back would give us an opportunity to make out.

We looked over the menu and made our selections. Collin, being the gentleman he was, ordered my food and drink. The second the lights dimmed, I removed my long sweater and draped it over my legs. I grabbed his hand and he willingly held on to it. Slowly, I moved my arm, bringing our hands to my lap. I waited patiently, praying he would make the next move, but he didn't. Trailers played for upcoming movies and he commented on them. I nodded and agreed. It took a concentrated effort to keep my focus off what I wanted him to do. Desire razzed my insides and I summoned the courage to take the next step.

I shifted and resituated my sweater so it covered our hands. He fidgeted and then leaned in closer toward me. Heat from the palm of his hand warmed my thigh and I tensed as a pulsating sensation shot up between my legs. I imagined his fingers touching me where I wanted him the most. My legs relaxed and my heart pounded inside of my chest. Inch by inch, I guided our hands up my leg, raising my skirt in the process. The roughness of his hand scratched against my skin and I took a few deep silent breaths as the movie began.

I kept my eyes focused on the screen, worried that if I looked at him, he'd pull away. For a long five minutes, I held this position, giving him the chance to act.

Surely, he knew what I wanted him to do.

The words Raven spoke to that girl on the phone repeated in my head and my pulse quickened. I squeezed my eyes shut, trying to focus on only Collin. Shifting my hand from underneath his, I pressed his hand firmly against my leg, splaying his fingers near my panties. He jerked his hand away in a swift movement at the same time the waiter appeared with our drinks. The only other time I'd seen him move that fast was on the field. Collin's hand collided with the tray the waiter held. Soda and ice flew in the air, half of it landing on my lap. I gasped, the sudden coldness extinguishing the sexual heat that flooded my veins.

"Oh, no! Are you okay?" Collin fumbled with his napkin, trying to unfold it.

"Sorry, ma'am." The waiter handed me a towel from his apron. "Can I get you some more napkins?"

I wiped my hands and then stood up, shaking off the ice cubes clinging to the lace on my skirt. "Yes, please."

People turned around and I felt horrible for interrupting the movie. How stupid was I to think that I could get Collin to touch me? My cheeks flushed with heat and I saw the regret in Collin's eyes. Regardless of my idiotic idea, a hint of happiness filtered through me because I couldn't help but wonder if the waiter hadn't appeared, would Collin have responded willingly?

Thankfully, the bathrooms had strong hand dryers so I was able to dry off without us having to leave. I hated that I missed some of the movie, but since I knew what happened, it was worth the short escapade. At that point, I was desperate and took what I could, just so I could experience something intimate between us.

He sat still the rest of the movie, keeping his hands to himself. I couldn't tell if he was mad or frustrated. After the movie, he maintained a safe distance from me as we walked to his truck, immediately crushing that hopeful thought I had after the spill. The ride back to the dorms was uncomfortable. I wanted to talk about what happened, but I was too scared to say anything.

As we neared the university, the lights from the football stadium shone brightly against the black sky. Was Raven practicing for tomorrow's big game? The more I tried not to think about him, the harder it was. I played with my engagement ring, sliding it half way off my finger and then pushing it back down. I did it repeatedly until my finger burned.

If it would have been Raven sitting next to me, I'm sure he would have given me an orgasm.

"Lexi?"

I jumped at the sound of Collin's voice. "Huh?"

Where the hell did that come from?

"I said I was sorry you missed some of the movie." Collin shifted the truck into park.

I stiffened at the sinful thought that had popped in my head. What was wrong with me? I was getting married! I shouldn't have been thinking things like that, especially about Raven.

Reason number four: Raven's clouding my mind.

"It's not your fault." I took a deep breath. In an effort to prove there was only one guy I should be lusting over, I turned toward him. "Do you want to come up?"

"To your room?" The hesitation in his voice squashed any optimistic thoughts of going further that night, but I refused to give up.

"Yes, silly," I laughed, trying to ease the tension building in the truck.

He glanced at the clock on his dash. "I better not. It's almost midnight. I need a good night's sleep so I can study all day tomorrow. I have a paper due and a test next week, not to mention practice on Wednesday."

"Okay." I heaved an audible sigh. "How about we study together tomorrow? Delaney went to the farm so it will be quiet."

He pressed his lips together and then smiled. "Sure. I'll be over around eleven."

"Okay." I inched closer to him, waiting for his kiss, hoping that my teasing had enticed him enough to want to kiss for a few minutes.

Instead, Collin opened his door and got out of his truck. Walking around, he opened the door for me. "I hope you liked the movie." He held out his hand to help me exit. His voice sounded so dry and distant that it made me question our relationship again.

"I'd walk you to your dorm, but I can't leave my truck here or they will tow it."

I forced a smile. "I know." I tilted my cheek in his direction and he gave me the customary peck. "Goodnight, Collin."

"Goodnight, Lexi."

The next morning, I ran around the dorm, cleaning and organizing my room along with the living room Delaney and I shared. I wanted everything to be perfect for today's study date. Going over the details in my head, I planned how I could seduce him in a way that he wouldn't be able to refuse me. Feeling the warning cramps of my monthly cycle, I pleaded with my body to give me just one more day.

I connected my iPod to my computer and quickly made a playlist of romantic songs. Then, I went to my closet and picked out a casual, but flirty outfit. Leggings paired with an off the shoulder, oversized shirt would be perfect. I chose a sexy black bra with matching panties and headed to the shower. Taking my time, I shaved any unwanted hair. I wanted my body to be silky-smooth for him.

After giving my hair a natural tousled blow dry, I grabbed my phone.

Me: Good morning, sweetie.

I had never given Collin a pet name, but I wanted to get to him. Make him tingle from his head to his toes. Five minutes passed before I finally received his text.

Collin: Sorry, just got out of the shower.

Me: Mmm, I wish I were there to dry you off.

That was the first time I had ever flirted that hard with him but I figured I'd better step it up. After a long wait, he finally responded.

Collin: I'm running a little late. I'll be there by noon. Would you like something to eat so we don't have to leave?

My heart sank. He didn't even acknowledge my playful suggestion. What would it take to get him to loosen up?

Me: Sure, whatever you want.

Collin: How about a turkey sandwich and chips from the deli down the street?

Me: Perfect.

I thought about telling him that all I wanted was him, naked in my bed, but that inner voice told me that might not be smart. I hesitated to put on any make up. Staring at myself in the mirror, I wondered if he would even notice. I shut the destructive thoughts out of my mind and decided to go with a natural look, spreading a smoky color across my eyelids and light blush on the apples of my cheeks. I finished with a fruity and sparkly lip-gloss.

Thirty minutes later, my phone dinged.

Collin: I'm downstairs.

Butterflies swirled in my stomach.

Me: Okay, I'll be right there.

I paced myself, walking instead of running down the hall to the elevator. Tingles danced up my spine and I hummed a familiar tune. I stepped out of the elevator and immediately caught a glimpse of my drop-dead gorgeous fiancé. He sported a pair of jeans and a blue and white striped sweater. My eyes traveled over his body. I couldn't wait to touch the muscles hiding underneath his layers of clothes.

"Hey, Lexi, you look pretty today... not that you don't look pretty every day." He flashed a grin and my heart melted.

He did find me attractive. Thank God!

"Aww, thank you. You look damn sexy," I said, observing him intently from head to toe.

His eyes widened and his head jerked back. "Oh. Thanks."

"Well, come on. I'm starving and I have a lot of reading to do." I grabbed him by the hand and started to lead him toward the elevators.

He wedged his hand from mine and stopped. "I think it's best if we stay downstairs to study." He dropped his backpack on a chair in the foyer.

The anticipation that was swelling inside of me vanished instantly. My shoulders sank and it felt like I had been doused with a thick layer of mud. I had spent all night obsessing over how to make our study date more intimate, but that would never happen if I couldn't get him up to my room. So far, things weren't working in my favor.

"I guess," I moaned. "I'll be back. I need to get my books." I dragged my feet all the way to my room. What was I thinking? Did I really expect him to race up to my room and rip my clothes off? I had to think of a better strategy to get us past home plate. I grabbed my backpack and headed downstairs.

"Here's your sandwich." Collin handed me a paper sack.

"Thanks." I sat the food on the table in front of me. I didn't feel like eating.

Collin settled in a chair opposite me, eating his food while reading. It was as though nothing had happened. Then again, he had no clue what I was trying to do. My main focus was getting him to show me how much he loved me and his was studying. Even though I needed to study too, I had to make sure I wouldn't regret walking down that aisle come June. I kicked off my shoes and tucked my legs underneath me, trying to think of a better solution.

Thirty minutes later, I opted for a different tactic. "Hey, Collin?"

"Hmm?" He looked up for a quick second and then zoned back in on his book.

"I was thinking about the wedding and what type of food we want served during the reception."

"Okay," he answered, but didn't appear very interested.

"What kind of food do you think we should have? Chicken or roast—" I stopping, waiting for him to respond, but he was too busy studying. "Or how about oysters on a half shell? We can also have a chocolate fountain and bathe ourselves in it."

"What?" His head popped up. "I'm sorry, Lexi, but can we talk about the wedding later? I really need to read this material."

I nodded as I recoiled into my chair. No matter what I did or said, Collin showed very little interest in me. I was striking out with every method I tried. If he didn't care to talk about the wedding, then did he really want to marry me? Was what Delaney said true? Was I his cover up?

A roar of laughter echoed across the room as a group of students filtered through the foyer. Collin shifted in his chair and exhaled, clearly perturbed that someone was disturbing his studying. Looking outside, I noticed the campus commons area fill with a rush of people. I glanced at my phone. The football game was starting in forty-five minutes.

Raven would be playing.

I slammed my book shut. "Hey, I have an idea."

He shuffled a stack of papers and then leaned forward, running his hand through his hair. "What's that?"

"Let's go to the game," I said with a cheerful voice.

He peeked from behind his hands. "What?"

I perched on the edge of my chair. "Yeah, it'll be fun. We haven't been to a football game this year."

"I know and I'm sorry. Between baseball, school, and the wedding, I haven't had time to think about football." He reclined in his seat and propped his leg on his knee.

"More reason as to why we should go. We both need a break from everything." I shoved my feet into my flats and started packing my books. "We're senior's this year, we should make the most of it."

He rubbed his chin as though considering my suggestion. "I'm sorry, Lexi, but like I said, I have a paper due and a test next week. I don't have time to go watch a football game. Maybe we can go to the last game of the season."

Irrational thoughts swamped my mind and I bit my tongue, forbidding any words that I might later regret to escape from my mouth. I shrugged. "I understand."

Darn, I really wanted to see Raven play.

Collin pulled another book from his bag and began flipping through the pages. I watched the students, smiling and laughing as they made their way toward the stadium. I wanted what they had.

Happiness.

Joy.

Excitement.

I hated that I never had the opportunity to experience *true* college life. I spent the first two years commuting back and forth to campus and what little extra time I did have I spent with Collin. When I moved on campus my junior year, I was too focused on my schoolwork, not to mention excited to finally be closer to Collin. Every time Delaney asked me to go out with her, I turned her down. I had Collin and was happy. Now, it was too late. And, I was getting married.

The crowd thinned and silence resumed over the empty dormitory and campus. It sucked that we weren't going to the game but that meant I still had a chance to get him upstairs. I walked over to the piano instead of reading my required literary fiction book.

"Hey, Collin, I realized we don't have a song." I hit a few chords, warming up my fingers.

"A song?" He looked in my direction.

"Yeah," I nodded, playing a stance from my parents' wedding song, *Endless Love.* "One we can dance to at our wedding."

"The one you're playing is fine." He returned his attention back to his schoolwork.

"No, that's my parents' song. We need our own song." I recalled another tune Delaney had asked me to learn. I ran over to my backpack and pulled out the sheet music. I studied it for a while, made some notations with my pencil, and did a light warm up with the main chorus and bridge.

"How about this one?"

I eased into the melody, focusing on playing the correct notes. As I continued to the main chorus, I gained more confidence and played louder. I waited for Collin to say something or recognize it because the radio stations had just started playing it. But he never did. Surely, he knew this John Legend tune. It was the most beautiful song.

Reading the words on the page, I imagined Collin singing them to me. He rarely sang so I had no idea if he could actually carry a note, but I didn't care. He could have sounded like a pig squealing and I'm sure my heart would have soared. If I wasn't so nervous, I would have bellowed the words, but my stupid throat tightened, fighting back the impending threat of tears.

I thought playing this romantic song might set the mood for my next plan of attack, but I was wrong. Before I could even finish the song, Collin began putting his books and papers in his backpack.

"What are you doing?" I immediately stopped playing.

Swinging his backpack over his shoulder, he said, "I'm sorry, Lexi, but I can't study here."

It felt like someone had pulled the rug from under my feet. "No." I rushed over to him. "Don't go. Stay here with me, please."

I had to do something, but the only thing that came to mind was to pull on the strap of his bag. The bag slid down his arm and dangled at his feet.

"We can go to the study room down the hall or the one on my floor." I scanned the room. "I think everyone's at the game so it should be quiet."

"Lexi," he huffed and looked a bit piqued at my reaction, "if you want to play the piano, that's fine, but I told you I have a lot of studying to do." He grabbed his backpack, holding it firmly in his hand by the strap.

His phone chimed. He pulled it out of his back pocket and scrolled through his phone. Sighing, he said, "Crap. I forgot that I promised my brother I'd take him to the batting cages tonight."

My entire body slumped to the floor. "Oh, I thought we could hang out and watch a movie or something."

"We went to the movies last night." He shoved the phone in his back pocket. Placing his hands on my waist, he said, "Why don't you come with us? It'll be fun."

"That's okay." I shook my head. "You know I'm terrible at hitting the ball." That was the truth. Luke must have hoarded that entire gene for himself because when it came to coordination, I had none. In return, I held the gene for being musically inclined and Luke couldn't hold a note to save his life.

"I'm sorry, Lexi. I'll make it up to you, I promise." Collin cupped my face with his hands and kissed me softly on the lips, causing my heart to warm, just a little.

Σ

Chapter 5

I sat in the writing lab, watching the minutes pass by as I waited for Raven. Part of me wanted him to show up while the other more reasonable part didn't. After last week's tutoring session, I wasn't sure if I could handle seeing him again or hear him talk dirty to another girl on the phone.

"Lexi, is everything okay?" Dr. Phillips approached me.

I grabbed my phone and shoved it in my backpack, forgetting that I wasn't supposed to use it while in the writing lab. A rule that I had allowed Raven to break.

Reason number five: I'm bending my own rules.

"Yes. I'm waiting on Raven to arrive." I tapped the end of my pen on the desk.

The professor shoved his hands in his pockets and jingled his keys while rocking on the heels of his feet. "I see. How did last week's sessions turn out?"

My stomach clenched. Did he really want to know? "Um, okay. Tuesday we reviewed one of his papers and I was able to help him identify some of his grammatical errors." Not to mention, he was able to give me a lesson on phone sex. One far more valuable than writing.

"That's great." He placed his hand on my shoulder and my body slumped down. "What about Thursday? I believe the agreement indicated you would be meeting him twice a week."

I couldn't even handle meeting him once a week, much less twice.

"Yes, that is correct. Unfortunately, he canceled our meeting last Thursday and is ten minutes late for today's session."

The professor frowned. "If he doesn't show up today, let me know. I will place a call to Coach Anderson. If we are doing this favor for him, the least he can do is show up and not waste your time."

I nodded. "I completely agree."

"Ah, look who's here."

I turned to see Raven walk through the door. He had on a PHU baseball cap, coupled with jeans that rode so low, if I had lifted his shirt, I would've seen his ass. My fingers twitched, eager to prove my point.

Dr. Phillips extended his hand to Raven and they shook hands. "Good to see you, Son. That was one heck of a game last week. You showed the Jayhawks we belong in the Big Twelve."

Raven adjusted his cap. "Well, what can I say? It was a close game, but we got in there and showed them we meant business."

"True, but in the end, we won the game. That's what matters." It was obvious that the professor was Team Raven, all the way. It wouldn't matter if I told him about Raven taking the sex call last week or if he continued to be a no-show or arrive late to every appointment. I was stuck helping him.

"Exactly." Raven crossed his arms and his muscles flexed. I instantly reasoned that I could be flexible and more understanding when it came to his schedule.

Raven turned to me. "Sorry I'm late. I had to go to the library and pick up a book I needed for a paper. I thought you might be able to help me with it."

The professor patted Raven on the back. "Good call. Good call."

He walked to his office and shut the door, leaving us alone in the center. Normally, it didn't bother me, but for some reason I didn't like that no one else was around. Maybe a part of me didn't trust Raven. Or worse, trust myself not to do anything stupid. I straightened and shoved off the silly thoughts teasing me to find out more about his sexual abilities.

"What do you want to work on today?" I arranged the papers in the folder Dr. Phillips had given me. I used them as a reference on the past work he had done.

"First of all, I want to apologize about last week." He took a seat next to me and pulled off his hat. He raked his fingers through his short, dark hair and I had to turn away to hide the fact that I was staring at him.

"Um, you want to apologize?"

He clasped his hands together and leaned against the table. "Yeah, ya know... the phone call last week." By the way the tips of his ears turned red and he fidgeted in his chair, I knew it wasn't easy for him.

"It's all right. Let's just forget about it and move on." I kept my eyes trained on his folder, refusing to give in to my desires that reminded me what he was capable of doing to me.

"Thanks." He bent his head down, trying to get my attention.

Cautiously, I peeled my eyes from the desk and gave him a slight smile. "Sure."

I swallowed the huge lump lingering in the back of my throat. Repeatedly, I told myself that I could tutor him. I was a mature, professional writing consultant that was engaged to be married. I had no business in philandering with him. I pulled my head back, straightened my shoulders, and pushed forward.

We had been working on an outline he needed help with for thirty minutes when his phone buzzed.

"My bad." He reached into his pocket and silenced his phone. A grin spread across his face as he glanced at the screen. He typed a text message and then waited a few seconds before typing a few more.

I strummed my fingers along the table as the minutes passed by. "Done sexting or do you need to leave so you can meet up with her?"

I figured it was the same girl from last week, or maybe a new one according to the report that Lisa Jenkins gave me when I called her last week. She wouldn't tell me much, only advised me to tread carefully and not to get involved with him. It was evident that the rumors about him having a different girl every week were more than likely true.

"Sorry about that." He shook his head. "She can wait."

A snicker escaped my mouth and I coughed to cover it up. Why did I care if he was sexting? I was still getting paid for my time, regardless. The more I thought about it, the more I wanted Collin to text me dirty and sensual messages. Too bad that would never happen. If I couldn't get him to touch me where I needed to feel him the most, how in the hell did I expect him to tell me what I'd like for him to do to me?

I gathered myself and continued helping him, extinguishing my inner desires. "I recommend that you do a comparative analysis of the two characters. It will add a more dynamic point of view and make it harder for your professor to argue the points."

He leaned back in his chair and scrubbed his face with his hands. "Damn, you really know your stuff."

I shrugged half-heartedly. "It's what I love to do. Just like you love to play football, I love to read and critique papers."

"I guess so." He raised a brow and I couldn't help but notice how dark his eyes looked against his black shirt. When I saw him last week, they appeared to be green; but that day, they looked brown. It seemed that he had hazel eyes, always changing, adapting to his surroundings. One thing was for certain, they were beautiful.

"Lexi?" Raven cleared his throat a few times.

"Yeah?" I shuddered, realizing I was daydreaming about him again. What the hell was wrong with me?

"I said, thank you for the suggestion. I think that's a great idea."

I tugged on the edge of my sleeves, trying to cover my trembling hands. Why the heck was I so nervous? "Oh, yeah, sure."

He gathered his books and papers and stuffed them in his bag. "I'll start working on it, and um... I guess we can review it on Thursday."

"Sounds good to me."

When he stood, a whiff of his cologne infiltrated my space. I inhaled deeply, to the point I thought I would pass out. I relaxed in my chair and watched as he adjusted his backpack over his broad shoulders. "See ya later."

"Yeah, see you later."

Σ

Chapter 6

My phone chimed and I rolled over, reaching for it.

Collin: I'll be there in thirty minutes to pick you up.

Blinking a few times, I struggled to see the time. Seven-thirty flashed on my phone. Collin was picking me up to attend weekly church service and I had over slept. Crap!

Me: Okay, I'll be ready.

I flung the covers off the bed and ran to the shower. Grabbing a hair band, I twisted my hair up in a messy bun and bathed as fast as I could. With little time to spare, I found a shear blouse and matching skirt that didn't need ironing and put it on. I applied a little makeup and ran downstairs. A few minutes later, my brother pulled up in his black 1969 Chevy Camaro.

The door opened and Collin stepped out of the car. "You look pretty in that skirt."

"Thanks," I said, ducking to get into the back seat. I didn't even try to kiss him. With my brother around, I knew he wouldn't be responsive.

"Hey, Bro, didn't know you were coming."

"Yeah, me either." He looked into the rearview mirror, brushing his thick, brown hair with his fingers. "Mom called and said they hadn't seen me in a while and... well, you know the drill."

I sighed and relaxed against the cold vinyl seat. "Yep, know all about that. Glad they're bugging you instead of me."

He laughed while peeling out. "Don't hold your breath too long, you'll be next."

"You know your parents mean well," Collin chimed in.

Luke's laugh deepened. "I can't wait to see what happens once you two get married."

"Oh, I don't think they'll continue to be overprotective. I know they want what is best for Lexi so they are willing to do whatever it takes to ensure she makes good decisions."

"Yeah, you don't know my parents as well as you think you do," I informed Collin.

"You might change your mind after a few weeks of my mom's nagging," Luke added.

"I think you two are wrong." Collin adjusted his seat belt but kept his body perfectly straight. "Not to be vain, but they know I'm a good choice for Lexi. They'll give us our privacy."

I had to bite back a laugh. Collin sounded so confident and cocky. If he only took that confidence into the bedroom, I might agree with him.

Luke slowed to a stop. "You might be the best guy for Lexi, but my parents will soon be telling you two how to live your lives. Trust me." Luke hooked his iPod up to his radio and turned on the music. The sounds of One Republic blared over the speakers.

The rest of the drive to Dallas remained quiet. I reclined my head, nodding in and out of sleep. My mind drifted off to Raven and our last tutoring session, but I forced the dangerous thoughts out of my head.

Reason number six: I can't stop thinking about him.

Church service seemed to drag and my stomach twisted with hunger pains. Since I was running late, I didn't have a chance to eat. The service ended and we made our way to the front entrance. Members gathered with their families, talking and smiling. Kids screamed and chased each other as their parents demanded they stop. I wondered if Collin and I would end up that way or if my display of marital bliss would be fake. Whether or not he was good for me, I was convinced that I needed someone who wasn't afraid to show me how much they loved me.

"Sweetie, how was your week?" Mom asked, smothering me with a hug.

I shrugged, hugging her back. "Okay, I guess."

"Collin, you always look so handsome." Mom gave him one of those hugs where she patted his back and kissed the air around his cheeks.

"Hello, Mrs. Thompson. You're looking younger every time I see you."

"Oh, thank you." Mom touched her hair and flashed a girlish smile.

Collin's phone chimed and he pulled it from his pocket.

"Lexi, my dad needs help with something. I'll meet you at the restaurant."

I nodded, "Okay."

"Excuse me, Mrs. Thompson," Collin gestured before fighting his way through the crowd.

"No problem." Mom waved but Collin was already deep in the throngs of people.

"You should have taken the time to fix your hair." Mom tucked a strand of hair behind my ear. "We're meeting the Norris family for brunch," she whispered. "You want to look your best."

"Sorry, I didn't have time." I adjusted my skirt, knowing she was checking to make sure I looked presentable. Whether I was fifteen, twenty, or forty, Mom would always nag about my appearance. "Where's Dad?" I asked, rising on my tiptoes to see over the crowds of people.

"He went to get the car. I told him I wanted to arrive at the restaurant early since they don't take reservations." Mom flipped her hair. "What do you think about this color? It's not too blonde, is it?"

Mom had light brown hair that was turning gray so she was testing different colors, claiming she had to have one that didn't make her appear too young or too old. "I think it looks natural."

"Good. It will be perfect for the wedding." She smiled and then her gaze darted behind me. "Luke! Oh, baby, come here."

Luke strolled behind the waves of people, in no rush to meet Mom.

"Hi, Mom." He embraced her while she planted a big kiss on his cheek.

"Sorry, baby," she said, her red lips staining his face. She licked her thumb, determined to rub it off. "When's the last time you got a haircut?" She immediately started messing with his hair.

Luke swatted her hand. "Stop, Mom. Leave my hair alone."

"Well your hair looks like that guy from Twilight."

"No it doesn't." Luke rolled his eyes.

"I think it does, so get a trim. And next time, don't forget to shave and iron your clothes..." Mom repeated her repertoire of dos and don'ts. It was nothing new and we were used to withstanding the brunt of her torture.

Luke managed to break away from Mom when she saw Dad pull up to the curb. "See you at the restaurant and hurry."

"Yeah, yeah, okay," Luke replied.

"We're right behind you and Dad," I assured her.

Luke and I walked to his car, taking the time to enjoy the nice, warm weather.

"Wow, it feels great out here." I took off my sunglasses and let the Texas sun beat down on my face.

"Better enjoy it now. It's supposed to get cold this afternoon."

"Darn, that sucks. I hate walking in the cold to class."

Luke unlocked the door for me. "Well, it's our last year so enjoy it before it's all over."

"Yeah, I guess you're right about that."

Since we were alone, I decided to ask him about Delaney. I waited for him to start the car and quickly took control of his iPod, turning down the volume.

"Hey, turn it back up. I like that song."

"I will in a minute, I just want to ask you something."

Luke's head tilted back and he rubbed his forehead. "Damn, Lexi, Mom's already beat me down today and I got an earful last night from Dad."

"About what?" Luke looked wiped and I questioned whether I should ask him about Delaney.

"Nothing." He pulled a cigarette from his visor and lit it. "Just baseball stuff... that's all."

I rolled down the window. I hated when he smoked, but I knew he did it to relieve stress. "If you need someone to talk to, I'm here." I swiveled in my seat, turning in his direction.

He flashed a quick smile. "Thanks, Sis, but its sports, and I doubt I'd hold your attention for more than a minute."

He was right about that. "Well, talk to Collin, I'm sure he'll be happy to listen."

He nodded, "Yeah, I will."

Turning up the volume to the music, I decided to give my brother a reprieve. We both needed a break and any extra crap could wait.

We walked into the restaurant and found Mom and Dad sitting at a big table. It didn't take long for the rest of the crowd to arrive. I greeted Collin's family and another couple my parents knew from church and their kids. Eager to distance myself, I sat at the very end of the table, opposite our parents. Collin sat next to me and my brother took a seat across from us. I listened to my mom make excuses as to why my sister and her family weren't at church, stating they had a mini-vacation to the Caribbean with some bigwig Dallas millionaire, and the kids stayed with their nanny. Mom always made it a point to talk about their rendezvous and whom they were rubbing elbows with if they weren't there. It was sickening.

Before I had met Collin, we only went to church on Easter and Christmas. When I started dating him, my mom made sure we were at service every week since Collin's dad was the pastor. Once we were engaged, Collin expected me to attend with him. I didn't mind, I just didn't prefer to wake up early on Sunday when I had to get up early the rest of the week. Saturday's were my only days to sleep in.

The waiter came by, took our drink orders, and informed us we could head to the buffet line. I ordered the usual, a Mimosa with an orange slice and cherry on the side. Mom and Collin's mom, Suzanne, did the same. Mealtime was the only time I was allowed to drink any type of alcohol. Collin's family only drank alcohol with their meals and my parents quickly adopted that same etiquette. Funny thing was, I remember Mom and Dad being big drinkers when we were smaller, but one day, they stopped drinking in front of us and taught us to drink only in moderation.

We hit the glorious layout of the New Mexican style food, loading our plates with various options. That was my favorite part of Sunday, great food and a nice, spritzy drink to melt away the week's worries.

"How's your food?" Collin wiped his mouth before taking a sip of his water. Collin rarely drank alcohol and if he did, it was a glass of wine.

"Good. How's yours?"

"Really good. The Adobe Pie is delicious."

I moved my fork toward his plate. "Can I try it?"

Collin moved his hand in front of his plate, guarding it. "I'll get you a fresh piece."

Seriously?

After all this time, he still refused to share his food with me. Yet he was preparing to share his bed with me. What the hell was wrong with him? What if he wanted us to have separate bedrooms like they did when my grandmother married?

"Sure," I said. Collin returned to the buffet line and I flagged the waiter. "I'll have another Mimosa, please," I said in a hushed voice. "And, can you bring it in a regular glass and not this fancy one?" I knew I wasn't supposed to drink another one, but since my parents were too busy chitchatting to notice, and Luke was engrossed with texting someone, I figured what the hell.

Collin returned with a fresh slice of Adobe Pie, but I didn't want it. I had wanted to taste his, but sharing food with me was something he obviously preferred not to do. Whatever the reason, it hurt my feelings. I kept to myself, not saying much of anything as my mind analyzed why I wanted to marry him. To make matters worse, Collin didn't even bother talking to me. He and my brother chatted the entire time about baseball season. Four Mimosas later, I felt numb and didn't care if we got married or not.

A cell phone chimed, and Collin asked, "Is that your phone or mine?" He lifted his phone out of the pocket of his blazer, giving it a quick glance.

I hiccupped and then flopped my purse on the table, searching for my phone. "Yep, it's mine," I roared. Several people turned and stared at me, including my mom.

Clutching my napkin, I covered my mouth, hiding the distracting noise that was a telltale sign that I probably had too much to drink. I didn't care. I liked the way the alcohol made my head feel, not to mention how it melted every muscle in my body. I made a mental note to drink at least two next time, but stop before four.

I held my phone close to my face and then moved it back, trying to focus on the text message.

Delaney: *So what happened? I'm dying to know.*
Me: *Shjt*

I set my phone down and flagged the waiter. Collin's eyes widened. Before I could say anything, he said, "Please bring her a big glass of ice cold water."

"Sure," the guy responded.

"How many Mimosas have you had?" Collin asked through gritted teeth.

I grabbed a fistful of his shirt, pulling him toward me, and planted a big fat kiss on his lips. "Enough to pull you into the bathroom and give you the ride of your life."

"Lexi," Collin muttered between our lips.

Luke started coughing and chortling as soda fanned across the table. "Darn ice... went down the wrong way." He pounded his chest, but the stunned expression on his face told me he must have heard me. I didn't care.

Mom's eyes narrowed and I swore I saw billows of steam blow out of her ears. Pastor Clifton didn't look too pleased either as his eyes darted between Collin and I.

My phone chimed again.

Delaney: WTF? Nothing happened?

My fingers pressed several keys at one time, but I managed to type a message to her.

Me: Nope. I tried to get him to touch men bit e got nervous and spit soda on me.

The waiter handed me a glass of water and I chugged half of it while waiting for Delaney to respond.

Delaney: What? He spit soda on you?

Me: No. Spilled. Damn autocorrect!

Delaney: That sucks. And yesterday? Tell me he spent the night.

Me: No.

Delaney: No, you're not telling me, or no, he didn't spend the night?

Me: He didn't stay. Said he had to story die.

Delaney: What?

I tried to type the right word, but my fingers weren't cooperating with my brain.

Me: Stuidy

Me: Stoody

Me: Shit! Study!

Delaney: Is this Lexi? Because she never has typos!

I giggled.

Me: Yes, it me. I drank four Mimosas.
Delaney: Holy SHIT! You're drunk!
Me: Yep. Feels good too!
Delaney: ROTFLMAO!

My phone buzzed as another text message appeared from a number I didn't recognize. I switched screens to read it.

Lexi, it's Raven. I need your help. Can we meet tonight?

"Shit! How did he—" I clamped my hand over my mouth when I saw all eyes gravitate toward me.

"Is everything okay, Lexi?" Irritation rang loud in Collin's voice.

"Sorry, I just forgot to do something." I waved a dismissive hand in the air.

Whispering, he said, "Please watch your language."

I nodded, not sure how to respond. My heart was pumping so fast I thought it would explode; not because of my Freudian slip but because Raven was texting me.

I zeroed in on the keys, making sure to type my message error free.

Me: How did you get my number?

Raven: Coach got it from Dr. Phillips. I hope that's okay because I REALLY need your help. I have a paper due tomorrow that I forgot about.

It wasn't okay because I never authorized Dr. Phillips to share my cell phone number. Typically, I only gave it to students I tutored if I thought it was absolutely necessary. It wasn't my fault he canceled Thursday's tutoring session again and failed to have his crap together. Even if the entire university wanted me to help him, I didn't want him to text me.

Or did I?

I hesitated for a moment, looking at my phone. My mind protested but something in my body welcomed the idea. A stampede of emotions coursed through my blood, awakening various extremities. Would he talk dirty to me? I pressed my lips together, forbidding the girlish giggle from trying to escape. There was only one way to find out.

Me: I guess. Can we meet at five?

Raven: That's fine. Where do you want to meet?

My phone buzzed again and Delaney's message appeared at the top bar of my phone.

Delaney: I'll be at the dorm later tonight. Visiting with family.

Me: Okay. Can't chat now. I'm talking to Raven.

Delaney: The football player?

Another messaged displayed from Raven as I was about to type back an answer to her.

Me: Yes, The Raven. The sexy football player.

Raven: Thanks. I'm glad you think I'm sexy. ☺

I looked at the top of the screen, seeing the name in the 'to' field. I had sent that message to Raven!

"Oh no," I gasped, pressing my phone to my chest. How could I have been so stupid? That's what I got for drinking and texting.

Delaney would love to hear about this. Should I tell her?

Using my better judgment, I decided not to. If she asked, I would tell her I was tutoring him. That was the truth, after all.

"Sis, is everything okay?" Luke asked.

"Yeah." The surge of adrenaline sobered me instantly.

Me: Sorry. You weren't supposed to see that.

*Raven: That's okay. *wink*

Oh my God! He winked at me. Cautiously, I typed back a message.

Me: Let's meet at the library at five.

Raven: See you then.

I stuffed my phone in my purse, deciding it was best if I stopped texting. I couldn't afford another screw up. Collin and Luke were back to talking baseball and everyone else was deep in various conversations, seemingly ignoring me again.

"I'll be back. I'm going to the restroom," I informed Collin.

He nodded, breaking eye contact with my brother for a quick second.

I stood and the floor tilted to the side. My head swayed and I gripped the chair for support. Placing one foot in front of the other, I made it to the restroom without falling. The walls of the stall seemed to move as I sat on the toilet. It reminded me of being in a fun house except it wasn't scary or spooky. I washed my hands, allowing the cool water to spill over my fingers. My body felt hot. I thought about dipping my head under the faucet, but I figured my mom wouldn't appreciate it if I came out looking like a wet mop.

I returned to the table to see everyone standing, saying their goodbyes. "We're leaving?" I asked Collin, gripping his arm for support.

"Yes, it's almost two."

"Darn, where did the time go?" I grabbed my purse and latched on to him.

He guided me outside and the bright light immediately blinded me. I released Collin's arm and reached into my purse, searching for my sunglasses. I slipped them on and walked toward Collin's parents.

"Goodbye, Pastor Clifton." I shook his hand, keeping a safe distance.

"Take care, Lexi," he said, squeezing my hand tightly.

Luckily, Suzanne cut in before I lost all feeling in my fingers. "Bye, Lexi. Oh, before I forget, I have a few photographers lined up for you to meet next Saturday at our house. Your mom said that would be fine."

I glanced at Mom and she smiled. Did anyone care to ask me? "Well, I was going to ask my friend Delaney to take pictures."

"Isn't she your maid of honor?"

"Um, yes. Yes, she is."

Suzanne adjusted her sunglasses and released a low laugh. "Then how will she take pictures, dear?"

The words jumbled in my head and I had trouble focusing. Damn alcohol. "I guess you have a point."

"Why not ask her to take some pictures beforehand?" Suzanne started walking toward the parking lot and I followed her. "I thought she was taking the engagement pictures?"

"Yes, she's supposed to." I quickened my step, trying to keep up with her. The next thing I knew, my foot slipped and I was airborne. My arms flayed to the side, seeking for something to hold on to but there was nothing. My butt hit the concrete, sending a sharp pain up my side. I lay on my back, sprawled on the sidewalk, crying out in laughter. Why I thought it was funny, I had no idea, but I couldn't stop laughing.

"Lexi! Are you okay?" Collin rushed to my side, helping me to sit upright.

"Oh my God, she fell." Mom covered her mouth and I started laughing harder.

The Norris' gathered around me, along with my parents. Collin's jaw worked back and forth and I knew he was withholding a few choice words. Why was everyone so uptight?

"What happened?" My dad's eyes narrowed and his nostrils flared. I knew he was mad at me, but more so because my mom would give him an earful all the way home. Poor Dad.

"I don't know... I was walking and I, um..."

"I saw it." Collin's younger brother, Shane, hovered over me, checking out the scene. "She wasn't paying attention and missed the step. She was too busy talking to my mom."

"Thanks, Shane, for that report," I grunted as Collin stood me to my feet.

"You didn't break anything, did you?" Mom asked in a curt tone.

"No." I dusted my hands and picked up my purse.

"But she'll have a big bruise in the morning." Luke flicked his cigarette and then pulled his keys from his pocket. "Let's go, I need to get back so I can study."

Mom's mouth fell open. "Why are you smoking? You know that will impair your abilities on the field!"

"So." Luke walked off and Mom scurried after him.

Mom didn't stop her lecture. "And why weren't you watching over your sister? I thought I told you—"

"I'm not her babysitter!" Luke got into the car and slammed the door shut.

Collin helped me to the car and I crawled into the back, pressing my face against the cold seat. It felt so good that my eyes fluttered closed on their own accord. I knew I had embarrassed my family and Collin, but it was unintentional. The drinks slid down effortlessly and they seemed to wash away all the worries about the wedding. No wonder people became alcoholics. The feeling was sort of addicting and I found that I liked it too much.

"Collin, can I talk to you for a moment?" Pastor Clifton stuck his head in the car.

"I'll be back," Collin said, before walking off with his dad.

"Damn, Sis. I can't believe you're drunk... and in front of your in-laws," Luke chuckled, shaking his head. "You've got balls girl. I'll give you that. Mom and Dad are going to rip you apart once you're sober."

"Don't remind me," I said, curling my body into a ball.

"Lexi?" Collin interrupted my dozing off.

"Yes?"

"I'm going home with my parents." He reached in the backseat and grabbed his backpack. Luckily for him, he never went anywhere without it. "They'll take me to my apartment later."

I sat up and my stomach turned. This couldn't be good. "Oh, okay."

"I'll text you later. *We* need to have a talk."

I thought about telling him that I had a tutoring session with Raven, but I didn't. The door slammed and he walked off.

Reason number seven: I'm keeping information from my fiancé.

Σ

Chapter 7

My phone rang and I covered my head with a pillow. A minute later, it chimed again, alerting me I had a message.

"Are you going to get that? It's gone off three times in the last ten minutes."

"Huh?" I peeked out from behind the pillow. My head throbbed with a vengeance, an obvious indication that I had too much to drink. Slowly, my vision cleared. I was on the couch at the apartment my brother and Collin shared with two other guys. I hesitated to look at my phone, figuring it was either my parents or Collin calling me. Neither of which I wanted to talk to.

I fished for my phone, finally pulling it from the bottom of my purse. I had three missed calls and five text messages. All from Raven.

"Crap!" It was fifteen minutes after five o'clock.

"What's wrong?" Luke asked, opening the refrigerator. "Mom's already calling?"

"No," I muttered as I quickly texted Raven that I was running late but would be there ASAP. "I...um, what happened?" I rushed to the bathroom in the hallway, praying that no one else was there.

"You passed out so I brought you here," Luke yelled. "And damn, you might be small, but you have one heavy ass."

"What? No, I don't." I slammed the bathroom door. After relieving my bladder, I took out a brush and combed my matted hair. I wiped the black from under my eyes, applied some lip-gloss, and then opened the door.

"Uh, you try carrying one-hundred and twenty-five pounds of dead weight up the stairs." Luke handed me a glass of water and an aspirin.

"Thanks. How did you know I needed that?" I swallowed the pill with a sip of water and then popped a piece of gum into my mouth.

He raised a brow. "I've been there before." Although I'd never seen my brother drunk, I knew that he wasn't as innocent as I was.

"Well, thanks for taking care of me. Is Collin here?"

"No. He hasn't made it back yet."

Thank God!

"Can you take me to the library?" I slipped my shoes on and straightened my wrinkled clothing.

"Right now?" He looked at his watch.

"Yes, I have a tutoring appointment and I'm late."

Tracking down the hall, he said, "All right. Come on."

The ride to the library was a few blocks away, but it would have taken me at least fifteen minutes to get there. We didn't say much and Luke didn't ask me any questions or give me an earful of his two cents. I guess he figured the lecture from my parents would be enough not to mention the *chat* Collin wanted to have with me.

"Thanks, Bro. Catch you later." I hopped out of the car.

"Later, Sis."

I hurried across the lawn and was surprised to see Raven sitting on a bench in front of the library. He glanced up from his phone and flashed a smile. My stomach flip-flopped. I had to admit; he looked super sexy in a leather jacket and faded jeans that had a big tear across the knee.

"Sorry, I'm late. I, uh..." I didn't know what to tell him. That I got drunk at brunch and had to sleep it off? Sadly, I'm sure he would've understood.

"Lexi?" His eyes narrowed in confusion.

"Yes?" I took a deep breath, unsure of why I was breathing so hard.

"Sorry, I didn't recognize you. You didn't have to get all dressed up for me."

Tilting my head to the side, I giggled. "Oh, I went to church this morning. I didn't have a chance to change."

"Oh, darn. I was hoping you were trying to impress me, you know, since you think I'm sexy." He winked at me.

A flash of heat burned my cheeks as his teasing captured every bit of my body's attention.

"Who doesn't think you're sexy?" The words escaped my mouth and I bit my lip, knowing I walked a fine line between flirting and being friendly. I knew what the fine print said about what was acceptable between friends of the opposite sex, but I was choosing to ignore it.

Reason number eight: I liked how Raven flirted with me and that was wrong.

His lips spread in a wide grin that revealed perfect white teeth. "Okay, now you're embarrassing me."

"Me?" I pressed a hand to my chest. "I didn't think that was possible."

"Oh it is, believe me." He stood and towered over my five-foot-five frame. "Well, you're thirty minutes late, so you owe me."

"Sorry. We'll work until we get the paper finished, even if it takes until midnight."

He inclined his head and we traded glances that yelled, 'Warning! Danger ahead!' but neither of us looked away. Instead, he held my gaze until I slipped deeper into dangerous territory. I tried to reel myself back in, but I couldn't seem to catch hold of anything. I was falling, emotions first, into The Raven's trap. And I didn't try to stop myself.

"Great, but first, let's grab a bite to eat. I'm starving and since we're going to be up late, I need some food."

"Sure," I agreed, knowing damn well that was the worst thing I could have done.

We walked to a taco shop on the opposite side of campus. My feet ached from the shoes I wore, screaming for me to take them off, but I managed to ignore it. Between the pain in my head and feet, not to mention, my heart, I hoped I wouldn't pass out again. I felt horrible knowing that I was probably ruining everything between Collin and me, but I was tired of being ignored. I needed someone who wasn't afraid to show me they loved me and I was tired of trying to please my parents. It was my life to live and I had to make sure I was making the right decisions.

"What would you like?" Raven stepped aside, allowing me to order first. I told the girl at the register what I wanted and took out my wallet.

"I'll get it this time. Next time, you pay," he said, pulling a wad of money from his pocket.

"Okay, thanks." Since Collin always paid, I kind of liked the idea of buying a guy lunch or dinner. Raven thumbed through several twenty and ten dollar bills. I thought about the stories I had read in the campus newspaper and wondered if they were true.

We got our drinks and sat in the center of the restaurant at a table. It felt weird not being with Collin, but I tried to relax and strike up a conversation.

"So, what's your major?"

"Business."

Oh no. Did he have any classes with Collin? "What year are you?"

"Sophomore, but I'll be a junior after this semester."

"Oh." I searched for something else to say but nothing came to mind. After a few moments of silence, Raven spoke up.

"I had to sit out a semester," he explained.

"It happens," I replied, acting like I knew other people that had to do the same.

"Hey, you want a beer?" He reached into his pocket and removed his ID. Curious to know his age, I slid it from his fingers.

Raven Renee Davenport
3029 Lubbock Street
Fort Worth, TX 76133

"Twenty-one. You just celebrated your birthday on September twenty-ninth?" I handed it back to him.

"Yeah." He shucked off his jacket and spirals of tattooed branches crawled up his right arm. His short sleeve shirt hid the rest of it and I found myself wanting to trace my finger along the curves to see where it led me. "Hey, you want a beer or a margarita?" He stood up.

"No, that's okay. I drank enough earlier."

"Seriously?"

"Yes." I bowed my head, keeping my eyes glued to the table.

"That's not why you were late, is it?" He leaned against the table, hovering close to me. His wonderful scent surrounded me and my knees weakened.

I played with the saltshaker, avoiding eye contact. "Yes."

He sat down. "I gotta hear this."

"You don't want to know."

"I love to hear drunk stories," he clasped his hand together, "especially when they effect me."

I laughed, but he kept a straight face. "Waiting."

"You really want to know?"

He nodded.

"After church, I went with my family to Blue Mesa for brunch and—"

"The one off of University Drive?"

"No, the one off of Northwest Highway in Dallas."

"Oh."

"Anyway, I had too many Mimosas and had to sleep it off at my brother's apartment."

He started laughing. "You got drunk off of Mimosas?"

I felt my height shrink about five inches. "Yes. They were really strong."

"So you're a light weight?" He turned when he heard our ticket number called.

"A light weight?"

"Yeah, you know... someone who gets drunk easily." He eased up from his seat.

"Well, I—"

"Hold that thought, I'll be right back." He pointed a finger at me while walking backwards to the counter. I laughed when his elbow collided with the back of a booth and he bellowed a cuss word. That was Raven, the bad boy that could charm the panties off any girl. But why had he resorted to drugs and drinking? He seemed like he enjoyed life too much. Maybe that was it. Maybe he didn't know when to stop or how to say no.

He placed my basket of tacos in front of me. "Thanks. They look delicious."

"Sure." He sat down and began eating his food. With a mouth full, he said, "So, if you get drunk off drinking Mimosas what does beer or tequila do to you?"

I shrugged and then wiped my mouth. "I don't know. Never tried them."

He took a drink of his soda. "You've never drank a beer or taken a shot of tequila?"

"Nope. Never have. I've only had wine and the champagne that's in a Mimosa."

"What year are you?"

"Senior."

He coughed, nearly choking on his food. "You're a senior?"

"Uh-huh," I said in between bites.

"Have you been at PHU all four years?"

"Yes." I smiled and then gulped down my water. Water had never tasted so good.

"So, you mean to tell me, you've been here for four years and you've never had a beer or a shot of tequila?"

I nodded while chewing my food.

"Wow. Do you live with your parents or something?"

"Nope. I live in Charter Hall with my friend, Delaney. My parents are really strict. They preached endlessly to me and my brother about never drinking, partying, having…" I stopped, not wanting to admit to the sex god that I was a virgin. That piece of information was vital to me. One mention of that and he'd probably have me on my back, right there on the table in the restaurant, in less than a second flat. The Raven would not be deflowering this girl. No way.

"Sounds like you were homeschooled."

"I was."

Raven's eyes widened and his light-brown skin turned a shade lighter. "My bad." He placed his hand on top of mine. "I didn't mean to offend you."

His rough hand melted my skin, rendering my arm useless. "It's okay. No offense taken." His hand lingered on mine a little too long, but I didn't mind. "It sucked. Believe me. And my parents still try to run my life."

"I see. Well, Lexi, sounds like you're a good person who's been brought up the right way." He finished off the last bite of his taco.

"Maybe. But I'm dying to experience life. I'll be graduating in May and I don't want to leave with all these regrets. It'd be nice to attend one party before I…" I trailed off, refraining from mentioning the word marriage.

Reason number nine: I'm totally avoiding the fact that I'm engaged.

He wiped his hands on a paper towel, wadded it in a ball, and tossed it into the empty food basket. "You've never been to a party either?"

I shook my head.

He pounded his fist on the table. "Damn, you are a good girl."

I crossed my arms and leaned back against the chair. "But I'm tired of being a good girl. I want to have some fun. I'll be twenty-one in March and I haven't experienced anything."

A big smile formed across his face. "That's spring break, baby. I may be—"

"The Raven's in the house!" A large husky guy hollered and hooted as several more guys trailed in behind him. They had to be part of PHU's football team based on their size.

"Hey, man, what's up?" Raven clasped hands with the guy and they exchanged a manly handshake.

They crowded around the table, some of them shooting a quick glance in my direction while the others didn't even notice me. I recoiled further into the chair, feeling the rise of testosterone in the air within the small restaurant. Never had I been surrounded by so much muscle, sweat, and eye candy.

I may need another drink to cool down.

Raven spoke with a few of the guys before they slowly dispersed, sitting in various booths. "Sorry about that, what were we talking about?"

I thought it was best not to re-enter the previous conversation, so I asked, "Are you from Fort Worth?"

"No. I'm originally from New Orleans. We moved here after Hurricane Katrina and decided to stay. You?"

"I'm from Dallas. I've lived in the metroplex my whole life." I scooped up the remains of my taco with a chip. "Alongside my sister and twin brother."

"You're a twin?"

"Yes. We're not identical, though." I shoved the chip in my mouth.

"No, shit." He crossed his arms and rested them against his chest. "I have two younger brothers. One's in high school and the other one is in middle school."

"Three boys. Wow! I bet that kept your mom and dad busy."

"Yeah, I guess." He shrugged and his eyes wondered off. "Oh, hell," he muttered.

Before I had a chance to ask what was wrong, a tall girl with blonde, stick-straight hair appeared at our table. "Trying to hide from me, Raven?"

Raven rolled his eyes. "Marcie, I told you—"

"My name is not Marcie, its Macy." She hiked her leg up in the air and using the heel of her shoe, she pushed him back in his chair and straddled him. Her butt scrunched against the edge of the table as she wrapped her arms around his neck.

Luke thought I had balls? This girl had balls and a vagina. And she was using them to her advantage.

Using both hands, Raven tried to peel her long slender arms from him, but she held on tight. "You never called me last night."

"Macy, can't you see I'm busy?"

"But you're never too busy for this." I leaned slightly to the right, trying to catch a better view of what she was talking about. She traced her pointed, black fingernail down his chest and then wiggled her pelvis, as though trying to turn him on.

Raven chuckled low in his throat as he shook his head. "You're too much for The Raven, you know that."

A low whimper coupled with a giggle sounded from her. "Call me later tonight?"

Placing two hands around her waist, Raven lifted her and placed her on her feet. "I don't know. I have a paper to write."

"Yeah, right." Macy crossed her arms. "Since when did you write your own papers?"

"Since a few weeks ago. Now, will you please leave us alone? We have work to do."

Macy turned in my direction and gave me a once over. She smirked and said, "I'd be happy to join you two."

"No, I don't think so."

Placing her hands on the table, Macy leaned forward, squeezing her breasts together to the point where they nearly popped out of her shirt. "Oh, come on. You know how much I love threesomes."

My jaw fell to the table. The girl had no shame.

Raven laughed. "Well, I don't know about that. I kind of like having Lexi all to myself." He shot me a quick wink. My heart stopped again and I had to take a deep breath.

"No fair." Macy batted her thick eyelashes at him and then shifted her shoulders, giving her boobs a nice little bounce.

"Sorry, I'm not up for sharing." Raven raised his hands and lifted his shoulders.

She pouted her light pink lips, and I hated to think about where they had been.

"Tell you what, why don't you go play with yourself first. That way, when I call you, you'll be nice and wet for me, okay?" He smacked her on the rear and she moaned as though she was having an orgasm.

Holy crap! Raven is just as bad as Macy.

"Anything for you, baby," Macy taunted before walking off to sit down with a group of girls at the back of the restaurant.

"Sorry about that."

Holding up a hand, I said, "It's okay." One thing was certain. The rumors about him being a ladies' man were true. Not only had I heard it first hand, now I'd witnessed it. Women were dying to get a piece of him and it only made me more curious.

Reason number ten: curiosity can be dangerous.

We walked to the library, neither of us saying much. I wasn't sure if he was embarrassed over the whole Macy situation or if knowing more about me pushed him away. Either way, it was probably for the best. I needed to keep a professional relationship between us. My contract stated that and since I really enjoyed working for the writing center, I didn't want to jeopardize that over a guy that would only take advantage of me. Raven wasn't worth it.

The main floor of the library was packed with students and the tension lingering in the air made it feel stuffy and confined.

"Do you want to try upstairs? The writing center has a meeting room."

With a shrug, Raven said, "Okay."

He followed me up the stairs to the small center. Sara and another consultant, whom I didn't know very well, worked with their students, not providing much space for Raven and me.

"I can ask them when they'll be finished."

"Nah, I'll find us a place." Raven took off in the opposite direction, weaving through the bookshelves. Standing with my hands on my hips, I sighed. Where was he going? He stopped, turned around, and motioned for me to come to where he stood. Sucking in a breath, I walked toward him. Off in the corner, was a small desk for one. Not the ideal writing set up, but a quiet spot, nonetheless.

"I never realized there were desks in this corner," I whispered.

He raised an eyebrow. "I know where all the private places are on this campus."

"Of course you do," I deadpanned.

Raven grabbed a chair from another table and set it down next to his. He removed his laptop from his backpack, along with his iPad mini, and handed me a piece of paper.

"That's what I've written so far."

"Okay," I replied, scanning over the few paragraphs.

"Are these your ideas for your paper?"

He propped his chin against his hand and swayed closer to me. "So far."

I kept my eyes trained to the paper. "The assignment is about *Maggie: A Girl of the Streets* by Stephen Crane?"

"Yep. I have to write a few paragraphs on a blog about it." I could feel the warmth of his breath spread across my face and neck as he looked over my shoulder. It made me shudder inside.

"Well, that's easy."

"If you've read it," he stated.

"What?" My head pivoted in his direction. With our faces only inches apart, my lips quivered, eager to meet his. I had to be crazy to think he would want to kiss me, especially after hearing how 'good' I was, but when his tongue slipped out, wetting his lips, I sensed that didn't matter to him. Maybe my good nature posed a challenge to him. Not wanting to seem desperate or like another one of his groupies, I refocused on the paper. I had a job to do. "So, you didn't read it?"

He shook his head.

Pressing my lips together, I searched for the right words. "Can I give you some advice?"

"Sure."

"Assignments are much easier if you read the material." I smiled and handed him his iPad. "I believe you can download it for free from Amazon."

"But I don't have time to read it." He took the digital tablet from my hand.

I looked at the clock on his laptop. "It's fifteen minutes until seven and it's a short story. I suggest you get started." I winked at him. "Can I give you another secret to successful writing?"

He heaved a big sigh. "What's that?"

"The more you read, the better you become at writing."

"Yeah, yeah. That's what the other tutor told me." Raven powered up his tablet.

"Well, it's true." I reached into my purse and pulled out my Kindle.

"What are you going to do?" Raven shifted in his chair, leaning against the wall.

"I have my own stuff to read for class. Don't worry about me, you just read that story and then we'll work on writing that blog. I promise, once you read it, you'll be able to write about it."

"Promise?" A smile played at the corner of his mouth, producing a slight dimple.

Tucking my hair behind my ear, I replied, "Yes. Now get started."

Three and a half hours later, we finished his blog post.

"Thank you so much for helping me." Raven held the door open as we exited the library.

"You're welcome. I knew you could do it once you read it." A strong gust of air wisped between the buildings, penetrating the sheer shirt I wore. "Wow! That must be the front my brother was telling me about." I wrapped my arms around my upper body, trying to block the cold.

"Where's your jacket?"

"I d-didn't bring one." My voice rattled in the wind. "I came from my brother's apartment, remember?"

"Oh, that's right." Setting his backpack on the ground, he pulled off his leather jacket. "Here, put this on."

What? Raven was giving me his jacket.

Holy crap!

"No, that's okay. It's a short walk to my dorm." My teeth chattered like it was fifteen below zero.

"Don't be silly." Raven held the jacket, waiting for me to put it on. "There's not an ounce of fat on your body to keep you warm."

Against my better judgment, I gave in and slid my arms through the sleeves. The silky lining covered my arms and body, cradling me in the smell of worn leather and Raven's tantalizing scent. Even though the jacket was three times too big for me, all I wanted to do was cuddle up with it and never take it off.

"What about you? It's freezing out here."

"Seriously?" He laughed. "I play football in colder weather than this."

"Yeah, I guess you do." I rolled up the sleeves, freeing my fingers but keeping it long enough to keep my hands warm.

"Come on, I'll walk you to your dorm." Raven motioned for me to follow him.

I hesitated for a moment, looking around campus. If someone saw me walking with him, word might get back to Collin. I didn't want that to happen. I was already in enough trouble after the Mimosa incident. "That's okay, you don't have to."

Raven stopped and turned toward me. "Lexi, it's almost eleven o'clock. I kept you out this late, the least I can do is walk you to your dorm."

He had a point. I never liked walking by myself this late at night. "Okay, I guess."

I walked hastily, looking around to make sure I didn't see anyone I knew. He kept up with me, one hand stuffed in his jean pocket and the other holding on to the strap of his backpack. Puffs of smoke escaped from our mouths as we tracked to the common's area. Just as we were about to cross the lawn, a guy on a bicycle zipped by me.

"Watch out!" Raven yelled. In one swift movement, he wrapped an arm around me and spun me to safety. His big, strong arms enveloped me and my head rested on his chest, like a pillow that fit perfectly.

Pressing a hand to his hard pecs, I gasped, "Thanks."

"Are you okay?" The brisk air swirled around us and he reached up, brushing my hair from my face.

"Yes." I smiled, slowly retrieving my hand.

It seemed like we stared at each other in the darkness of the night for hours, but I knew it had to only be a few seconds. Slowly, our eyes broke away and we continued up the walk.

Stopping at the main entrance, he said, "See you Tuesday?"

I nodded and waved bye, unable to tear my gaze from his charming smile. If only Collin would look at me that way. I sighed and walked into the dormitory.

Reason number eleven: Raven's stealing my heart.

Σ

Chapter 8

My feet floated effortlessly with each step I took. Feeling lighter than air, I wanted to spin across the shiny tiled floor, but I imagined that the couple sitting on the couch would laugh at me. Raven sure knew how to leave an impression, even if it was unintentional. Instead of going upstairs, I approached the couple.

"Do you mind if I play the piano?"

They traded glances as though reading each other's mind. "No, go ahead," the guy said.

"Thanks."

I sat at the piano, noticing my music sheets from the day before were still perched on the music rack. At first, I hesitated to play the song, recalling how Collin failed to take notice. My throat tightened, but I swallowed back the pain, refusing to shed any more tears over him. I watched the couple in the corner snuggle and nose kiss and decided if the song wasn't right for Collin and me, then maybe it was perfect for them.

My fingers pressed the white and black keys, bringing the chords to life. I hummed the words under my breath, longing for the love that John Legend sang about. By the second chorus, the couple approached the black baby grand and embraced. Maybe one day a man would love me unconditionally and not be afraid to show it — like the way that guy was expressing to his girlfriend. It was the sweetest compliment to be able to play for someone and have them truly appreciate it. Even if Collin didn't, I wouldn't let that stop me from enjoying something I loved to do.

After I played the last notes of the song, a burst of clapping erupted through the foyer. I looked at the couple and they both responded, 'thank you', but neither of them had clapped.

I turned around, searching for my admirer and was shocked to see Raven standing a few feet behind me.

"Raven. How long have you been listening?"

"For a while." He approached me. "You didn't tell me you played the piano."

I vied for an explanation. "Um... I didn't think to tell you."

"You are truly gifted, Lexi." He crouched next to me.

The familiar flush of heat reappeared. "Thanks. I really enjoy playing."

"Don't stop, because that would be a waste of talent."

I giggled. "Is that your line or did someone tell you that?"

"Both," he grinned.

"Don't take this the wrong way, but why are you here?" I clasped my hands together, wiping the sweat from my palms.

He tugged on my sleeve. "I forgot my jacket."

I glanced down. "Oh no, I'm sorry." Slowly, I began to remove it, but before I could slip off the jacket, he stood and eased it down my arms. Chill bumps dotted my skin and I was glad I had on a long sleeve shirt, even though it was sheer.

"It's okay, but since it's the only jacket I have right now, I need it back. I'll have to grab another one from my mom's house."

"No problem," I smiled.

"Can you play anything else besides *All of Me*?"

Oh my god! He knows John Legend.

I laughed. "Yes, lots of songs."

"Would you mind playing a few for me?"

The air left my lungs in a rush as I sat perfectly still, looking at him. My body flanked on the edge of hyperventilation. If only Collin would take an interest in my musical ability.

He held up his hands in surrender. "It's okay, if you don't want to."

"No!" I gasped. "I mean yes. Yes, I'd be happy to."

He eyed me. "Are you sure?"

"Yes, I'm sure." I squirmed in my chair, trying to find a comfortable position. "It's just that I rarely have anyone ask me to play for them, other than my roommate and family."

"Well, I love the piano." He pinned me with his fascinating hazel eyes, propelling me into another daydream.

Clearing my throat, I said, "Have a seat, Raven." I scooted to the edge and patted the space next to me.

He lowered to the bench and my body hummed with desire. "How long have you been playing?"

"Since I was ten." I pressed several keys simultaneously, playing the bridge from Bella's Lullaby.

He pointed at the keyboard. "I know that song. That's um..."

I continued playing, loving how he tried to recall the song.

"Don't tell me... it's from that vampire movie. Twilight!"

I laughed again. His reaction was priceless. "You know Twilight?"

"Who doesn't? Besides, my mom was one of the Twi-Moms or whatever you called the mothers who followed the books and movies."

I stopped playing. "Your mom sounds cool. Unlike my mom." I heaved a sigh. "I tried to get my mom on board but she never took an interest."

He shrugged. "You can't win them all."

I'd sure like to score with you.

What's wrong with me?

I elbowed him, trying to distract my wondering mind. "Name a song."

He cocked a brow at me. "Any song?"

"Preferably one that is dominate piano." I allowed my deft fingers to scroll along the keys.

"Lean on me."

"You've got it." Keeping my eyes steady on the keys so I didn't get distracted, I played the intro. By the time I reached the first verse, we started swaying to the left and right, following the beat of the music. In a low voice, I sang the words and within a few seconds, Raven joined in. To my surprise, he had a great voice. Before I knew it, we were bellowing the words at the top of our lungs, looking at each other as we chanted the lyrics as though we were lifetime friends.

In a hushed voice, with eyes fixed on one another, we sang, 'just call me, call me, call me' repeatedly as the song dwindled to an end. The emotions exchanged between us hit me like a tidal wave and I struggled to keep it together. Never had I experienced something so intense and fun at the same time. The relationship building between Raven and I was nothing like I had imagined. It was so much more than the relationship Collin and I had. And, I had known Collin for more than half of my life.

Raven tilted his head to the side and his brown eyes appraised every part of my face with soft detail. Did he really want to kiss me? My body tensed and my heart pumped fast as I prepared for his lips to meet mine. I didn't want to hurt Collin, but I was losing the fight, desperate to feel love. Face to face, the air stilled between us, and I pressed my lips outward. Raven's lips parted and just as we were about to kiss, his phone buzzed.

Startled by the vibration, I jumped back.

"Sorry," he smiled as he fumbled to pull his phone from his pants pocket.

I tried not to look at the screen, but my eyes drifted naturally. It was Macy. My body slumped forward and all traces of happiness and excitement instantly vanished. I had to be crazy for thinking Raven was interested in me. After all, I was in the peewee league and Macy was a top hitter in the pros.

Tucking the phone in his back pocket, he said, "I need to go."

"Booty call?" I said with a snarky tone. He busted out in laughter as he dragged a hand over his mouth. I kept a straight face, purposely.

His laughter waned when he saw that I didn't find amusement in my comment. "Do you really want to know?" His voice had a disdaining tone and I reminded myself what The Raven was known for.

I'm such an idiot.

"Hey, whatcha doing?"

I turned at the familiar sound of my roommate. "Delaney, I, um... was just, we were..."

"I was just leaving." Raven stood up.

Delaney looked at Raven and then at me. I had to say something before any questionable thoughts could form in her mind. "This is Raven Davenport. Raven, this is my roommate, Delaney."

They shook hands and I watched Delaney give her classic introduction of batting her thick eyelashes coupled with a sexy twitch of her shoulder.

Half a minute later, she said, "Oh, you're Raven. The football player."

He inclined his head. "Yes, among other things."

The flirting never seemed to end. And to make matters worse, Delaney was falling for his antics, too. I knew if given the opportunity, she would gladly toss her panties at him. Hell, if I had to guess, she wouldn't even wear any.

"So I've heard..." she trailed off in a girly giggle.

Raven put on his jacket with finite moves and I struggled not to watch every muscle flex underneath his cotton Henley shirt. He flipped the collar down and glanced at me with an impish grin. "See ya Tuesday?"

As much as I hated to give in, I found myself smiling back at him. The guy was freaking irresistible. "Yeah, see you then."

Delaney and I stood, shoulder to shoulder, waving as the gorgeous hunk walked out of our dormitory.

Reason number twelve: I like the way Raven makes me feel.

"Holy shit." Delaney flung around and latched on to my arms. "What was he doing here?"

"He forgot his jacket."

Her eyes widened. "What?"

"Ow. Nails." I pulled away. "You're digging your nails into me."

"Oh, sorry," she said, releasing her grip.

I looked around and saw a few students sitting in the corner with their books spread across a table. Even if they were studying, I didn't want to take a chance. "I'll tell you upstairs." We walked toward the elevators.

"You're getting back late from Greenville." I glanced at my phone and it showed fifteen until midnight. "Where's your stuff?"

"Oh, I...uh...got back around eight but grabbed a bite to eat with a friend." She crossed her arms and turned around, avoiding eye contact with me. I knew she'd done more than go out to eat.

"You should have at least brushed your hair and fixed your makeup," I teased.

"What?" Delaney used the camera on her phone to finger-comb her sex hair and check out her swollen lips and full beard blush.

"Come on, who were you with?" I nudged her as the elevator doors opened and we stepped in.

"Huh? No one. It's windy outside." The elevator doors shut and she quickly changed the subject. "Why did you have Raven's jacket? And why were you two texting earlier today?"

"I went—"

"And why were you drunk? I mean, that's good, you're finally loosening up. And what about Collin? Are y'all still together?"

"Laney!" I motioned for her to stop. The doors opened and I bailed out, pulling her with me as I made a beeline to our rooms, not giving her a chance to ask anything else.

I unlocked the door and we stumbled in the room. "Tell me. I'm dying to know."

Falling on the couch, I grabbed a throw pillow and clutched it to my chest. "Let's see, I'm not supposed to tell you this because of client-student confidentiality—"

"I promise, I won't say anything."

With hands on her hips, she stood waiting for me to say something. "I'm tutoring him," I finally admitted.

"What?" She sat down beside me, crossing her legs underneath her. "You're tutoring Raven Davenport?"

"Yes, as of two weeks ago." I picked at the nail polish on my nails, determining what I should or shouldn't confess. "It wasn't my choice, believe me. Dr. Phillips practically forced me to help him."

"Damn, you're so lucky," she sighed as her eyes glazed over.

I started laughing at the expression on her face and it didn't take long for her to join in. "Okay, I'll admit that he is damn fine and he makes me so nervous. But honestly, once you get to know the guy, he's really fun."

"Yeah, I saw that."

I gasped, releasing the pillow from my death grip. "Saw what?"

She waved a dismissive hand in the air. "Relax. I heard y'all singing your hearts out as you played. At first, I didn't think it was you because I didn't recognize the guy, but as I waited for the elevator, I zoned in and realized it was your voice. When I went to see, you had stopped and that's when I approached you."

I sucked in a deep breath. "Oh, good."

"Why, did something else happen? Oh. My. God. You didn't kiss him, did you?"

Giving her a less than playful slap on the arm, I said, "Of course not."

She shrugged. "Hell, I would've."

I rolled my eyes. "Yes, I know you would have. But did you forget," I sighed again, "I'm engaged." I held up my left hand, showing her my ring. Then, it dawned on me. Had Raven seen my ring? If he did, he didn't say anything about it. Then again, maybe he didn't care.

Lowering my hand, she shot me a meek smile. "Tell me everything. I want details."

I pivoted my body and faced her. Once I got started, I couldn't stop. I spilled my guts, sparing no details from the time we met until tonight. It was a relief but nerve-wracking at the same time. Never had I been so honest with her, but I couldn't keep this to myself any longer. I needed a sounding board with someone that had experience with guys. Delaney was more than qualified. I even explained how I had continued to entice Collin, and without fail, how he pushed me away.

"I'm a horrible person." I buried my face into my hands, feeling the pangs of guilt rush over me. "Collin's a good guy."

Removing my hands, she said, "Yes, he is and you need to have a come to Jesus talk with him because what you've been doing isn't working. I already told you, if you don't have an unfailing love before you get married; you'll end up miserable and eventually divorced."

I nodded. "I know. I owe that to him." I picked up my phone, noticing I had two missed calls from my parent's house but nothing from Collin. "He wasn't very happy about me getting drunk and falling at the restaurant today. He said we needed to have a chat, but he hasn't bothered to call or text me."

"Looks like you're going to have to take the initiative."

"I guess." I sat my phone next to me.

"But I will admit one thing."

"What's that?" I peeked at her through the strings of hair hanging in my face.

"I've never seen your eyes sparkle like the way they did when you were talking about Raven."

"What?" Heat swamped my face.

"It's obvious you like him."

I closed my eyes and tried to convince myself that I didn't, but the heat only intensified and the smile refused to go away.

"If a guy makes you that hot and bothered, then there's no denying it." I opened my eyes and shrugged. "But I'm going to warn you, Raven has a bad rep and he's probably not the best guy to fall for, that is, unless you're just looking for some dick."

I coughed, choking on my spit. "Laney!"

She held up her hands. "Just saying."

Not once had I thought about his penis, but now that she'd mentioned it, I couldn't help but wonder what was hiding in those jeans of his.

"I'm sure he has plenty of it too... mm." She rubbed her hands together like she was preparing for a feast.

"Stop." I fell onto the mounds of throw pillows behind me. "You're killing me," I cried in between laughs. "Man, it's been one hell of a day." I heaved another big sigh.

She stood and tossed a throw pillow at me. "But it's been your best day yet."

Before I went to bed, I typed Collin a long text, pleading for him to forgive me. I stayed up half the night, tossing, and turning as I waited for him to reply but he never did. At seven-thirty the next morning, I received a call from my mom. She lectured me for at least half an hour as I made up excuses for my inappropriate behavior. I waited impatiently for Collin to acknowledge my message, checking every few minutes as I kept her on speaker mode. I wished my mom and I had a relationship where I could talk to her openly about things, but we didn't. She wouldn't understand what I was going through with Collin. In her mind, he was the perfect guy for me and could do no wrong. She might have been right, but unless he showed me that he loved me, I wasn't convinced.

As soon as she hung up, I rushed to shower so that I could make it in time for my nine o'clock class. It was the only class Collin and I had together and although I dreaded seeing him, I knew avoidance wasn't going to solve anything. I put my clothes on, grabbed a cereal bar and a glass of juice, and rushed to get ready.

As I dried my hair, I kept a steady eye on my phone, waiting to see if he would respond. But my text was the last thing shown on the screen. I applied a little makeup, not caring if I looked like death because nothing would hide the dark circles. I slipped out of the dorm, careful not to slam the door and wake Delaney. I walked across the lawn, still checking my phone every few minutes until I entered Scholar Hall. The building buzzed with students, rushing to arrive to their class on time. I zipped my way through the crowd, eager to talk to Collin before class started.

Sitting in his usual spot, Collin kept his face down, nose deep in a book. Easing into the seat behind him, I kept quiet, waiting to see if he would speak first. He didn't.

I leaned forward and whispered, "Collin, did you get my text?"

His head rose, but he stayed facing the front of the room. He gave a slight nod and then returned to reading his book. I slumped against my chair. In the six years that I had known him, I had never endured this much silence. There was one time we had argued about me working once I graduated if he happened to land a baseball contract and that didn't end well. He gave me the silent treatment for a few days. I figured that my Mimosa episode would garner the same kind of response, if not worse.

Professor Garza walked into the room and placed his bag on the chair. A hush fell over the room as he began to speak in

Spanish. I waited patiently to see if Collin would text me during class, but he kept his attention on the instructor the entire time. I thought about tracing my name on his back with my finger, but reasoned with myself that would've been a bad idea.

An hour later, class ended and the students filed out of the room in a rush, including Collin.

"Hey, Collin, wait up." I tossed my books in my bag and tracked after him. "Slow down," I called after him but he continued to ignore me. "Can we talk?" I said, finally catching up to him.

He kept walking, not bothering to make eye contact with me. "Right now is not a good time, Lexi."

I zipped up my jacket, protecting myself from the brisk breeze as I tried to keep up with him. "It seems like you never have time for me."

He stopped suddenly. "Sorry, school and baseball are my first priority."

I felt a piece of my heart crumble, but I managed to keep the tears from falling. "I thought I was supposed to be first."

He shifted and let out an audible sigh. "You make it really difficult for me."

"I'm not trying to. All I want is your love, can't you see that?" I pleaded with him.

"And you have that." A perplexed expression formed across his face.

"But I don't see it or feel it." I searched his face for any trace of a sign. "I feel like we're just friends."

"What?" He moved to the side, allowing a few students to pass. "I'm working my butt off, trying to land a contract with a team, not to mention do well in school in case that doesn't happen, all to support you." His green eyes flared a deeper color. "If that's not showing you how much I care for you, then you must be blind."

"Thank you, I appreciate all that you're doing for us." I reached for his hand, but he jerked his hand away. "Please don't touch me right now."

"Okay, fine." I crossed my arms. "All I'm saying is I need to feel your love, so a little attention would be nice."

"Is that why you got drunk? To get my attention?"

I shrugged and stared at the ground.

"Because that's the wrong way to get it," he huffed. "My parents are very disappointed in your behavior and so are your mom and dad."

"You called my parents?"

He glared at me openly. "Yes."

"How could you?" My stomach hardened. I couldn't believe he did that. I didn't want to think about the conversation he had with them because doing so made me so much angrier.

He stepped closer to me. "You need to stop and think about what you did."

"I'm sorry, but couldn't we have discussed this instead of you calling our parents? I'm not a kid, Collin." I needed a partner not another parent. I swallowed repeatedly, but couldn't stop the tears from forming.

"I don't know what's gotten into you lately, but I don't like it one bit." He held his chin high.

"You don't like me coming on to you?"

He took a deep breath. "This was never a problem before, what's changed?"

"I want more from you." Tears dripped from my eyes. Was coming on to my fiancé that wrong? I knew I shouldn't have drank in front of his parents, but the stress of our relationship was becoming more than I could handle. I felt lonely and confused. The alcohol seemed to take that away.

"How can I want a drunk and sex crazed woman?"

"But I'm your fiancée." I wiped the tears away.

"Then act like it." His tone deepened and it reminded me of my father. He sighed heavily. "I have to go. I'll call you later."

He left me standing among the hordes of students, crying my heart out. Several people turned and stared, but I didn't care. I knew that getting drunk was wrong and flirting with Raven was a huge mistake. In all honesty, Collin and I had started drifting apart before I met Raven. All Raven had done was made me realize what I was missing in my relationship with Collin.

If only Collin would open his heart and allow me to love him. None of this would be happening.

I wasn't convinced anymore that I belonged with Collin.

Σ

Chapter 9

The rest of the day dragged and I questioned everything that had happened since I met Raven. It was reassuring to know that Collin was working hard to secure a future for us, but it still didn't change the fact that I needed to feel love from him. Otherwise, what future would we have? I needed to experience a certain level of intimacy with him that reassured me that we were more than friends. Of course, I wanted hot, sensual sex with him before we tied the knot, but if I couldn't have that, I at least wanted some tempting make out sessions with him. Surely, he wanted the same.

Later that night, Collin apologized for the way he acted. He asked if I could give him a few days to himself so that he could finish his paper and study for his test. I offered to proof his report, but he turned me down, saying that he could do it himself. It bothered me that he refused to make a little time for me. The next day I ignored his request and asked if he'd like to meet for a quick bite or if I could come over and cook him dinner. He declined, stating he really had to study since he had practice on Wednesday and his test was Thursday. It proved to me that what he said was true: school and baseball came first.

Raven canceled our Tuesday tutoring session claiming he needed to read the material before we met. It made me happy to see that he was taking my advice, but I hated to admit that I was slightly disappointed. However, I knew it was for the best. I had to get my head straight and decide if I wanted to be with Collin. I was glad that I had told Dr. Phillips to reassign my other two students. I definitely had too much going on with school, Collin, and now, Raven.

Delaney hated that Collin and I were still at odds with one another, but was glad to hear that I wanted to keep some distance from Raven. She thought that giving Collin some space was smart but told me that I should have another talk with him. She reasoned with me that his lack of affection was probably due to his nonexistent experience and that he was introverted. I reminded myself of those things daily, especially when I didn't hear from him, even though I knew he wouldn't call me until after his test.

Thursday's classes were over before I knew it and I tried not to get excited about my tutoring session with Raven. As I headed out of Ramsey Hall, several men rushed past me carrying industrial size shop-vacs and large fans. I didn't think anything of it and texted Delaney to meet me at the sandwich shop located by the campus. A missed call flashed across my screen. I called my voicemail and listened to the message. It was Dr. Phillips, stating that a pipe had busted in the bathroom and flooded the writing center. That explained why the men were running through the building. I hesitated to text Raven, but I had to inform him so we could find an alternative meeting location.

Me: Hey, Raven, the writing center is flooded so we have to find another meeting place. How about the library?

I shoved my phone in the outside pocket of my bag and walked down the street.

"Lexi," Delaney called.

Turning, I saw my roomie a few feet behind me. I waited for her, thinking of some meeting places.

"Are you done for the day?" she asked in an overly cheerful tone.

"With class, but I have to meet Raven for his tutoring session."

"Uh oh." She eyed me and I felt my blood quicken in my veins.

"What?" I held up my hands. "I have to tutor him."

"Just be careful." She held the door open and we entered the restaurant. Only a few tables were taken so I knew we had beaten the lunch crowd.

My phone chimed and I retrieved it, seeing that it was Raven.

Raven: No problem. But I don't like meeting in the library.

Me: Okay. We can meet at my dorm, there's a study room downstairs.

Raven: That's fine. See you in an hour.

"Look at you." Delaney peeked at my screen. "You can't stop smiling while you text him."

"Stop," I whined and then pulled my phone from her view. When I realized I was smiling, I relaxed my face. I quickly sent Raven another message.

Me: See you then.

"We had to discuss where we would be meeting since the writing lab is flooded," I explained.

Delaney told the guy behind the counter what she wanted before responding to me. "So where are y'all meeting?"

"In the downstairs study room of our dorm," I replied, tucking the phone away.

She spun around. "You are? Damn..."

I waited for her to continue but she didn't. Instead, she walked off to find a place to sit. I ordered my food and then joined her in the booth. She was busy texting and I noticed she kept the phone tilted up so I couldn't see whom she was chatting with.

"Is everything okay?"

"Yep." She glanced up quickly, still texting. She stared at the screen for a few seconds and then tossed her phone in her backpack.

"Who was that?" I asked as she got up to get the food.

"No one. Just a friend." She scurried off, not giving me a chance to ask her anything else. I knew she was hiding something.

"Thanks." I took my tray from her.

"Sure." She sat down and unwrapped her meal. "Hey, do you and Collin have any plans this weekend?"

I shrugged. "Not that I'm aware of. Why?" I took a bite of my sandwich.

"Well, Jordan and I were thinking about getting a group together to go bowling."

"That sounds like fun." Jordan was one of Delaney's friends. She was also dating Forbes, another baseball player that lived with my brother and Collin.

"Ask Collin and see if he's up for it."

I swallowed. "I will when he calls me."

"He still hasn't called you?" Delaney asked with a mouthful of food.

I shook my head. "I'm sure he'll call me today after his test." I could only hope.

"Don't you have class with him on Tuesdays and Thursdays?"

"Yes, but he wasn't there today." I took a drink of my water, trying to push down the lump quickly forming in the back of my throat. "If we go out, it'll have to be Friday night because he doesn't prefer to go out on Saturday nights since we have to get up early on Sunday."

"Yeah, yeah, I know." She wiped her mouth. "Friday's fine."

My phone chimed and Delaney raised her brows.

"It's Collin," I said, glancing at my phone. "He probably just finished his test." My heart skipped a beat, hoping he wanted to hang out.

Collin: Hey, Lexi, just completed my test. It was a tough one. Thank you for giving me some time. I really needed it and I hope we can move forward.

He may have needed it, but I needed him more. I considered telling him that but decided to save that for an in person conversation.

Me: I'm sure you got an A.

A few seconds later, he replied.

Collin: I hope so. I wanted to take you out to dinner tonight but my dad called and asked that I go home. He wants to talk to me about a mission trip.

My heart sank.

Another excuse.

Did his dad really want to see him? Was he making this stuff up? Why didn't he invite me to go with him? Giving him the benefit of the doubt, I texted him back.

Me: It's okay. I have a tutoring session and a test to prepare for next week. You can make it up to me, though. Lexi and Jordan want to get a group together to go bowling on Friday night.

"Is everything okay? Looks like someone kicked your dog."

I shook my head. "Collin has to meet with his dad tonight, which means we can't hang out."

She reached for my hand and I clasped on to hers. "I'm sorry."

Tears threatened to escape once again and I fanned my eyes. "Don't cry."

I pressed my lips together. "I'm not. It just really sucks because I'm trying so hard."

"I know you are. I still think you two need to sit down and have a serious talk."

"I know. He did say he wants to move forward."

Dipping her potato chips into ketchup, she said, "I guess that's a good sign."

My phone chimed again. I hesitated to read the message, convinced that he had another excuse.

Collin: That shouldn't be a problem. I'll check my schedule and let you know. I'll call you when I get back to the apartment later tonight.

Me: Okay. Be careful and call me as soon as you get home.

Collin: I will.

I sucked in a deep breath. "He says he'll check his schedule and let me know later about Friday."

"Um, that's tomorrow night."

"You know Collin. He has to check his schedule before committing to anything. But if he says no, I'll go regardless."

Delaney shoved another chip in her mouth, dripping with ketchup.

"That's disgusting, you know." I took another bite of my food.

"It tastes so good." She licked the residue off her fingers. "It'll suck if he says no."

"Yeah, but what can I do?" I picked up my phone and noticed the time. "I gotta go." Gathering my trash, I tossed it on to the tray. "I'm meeting Raven in ten minutes. I'll catch you later." I grabbed my stuff and headed for the door.

"Hey, Lex," Delaney called.

"Yeah?"

"Don't give up yet, he's a good guy."

Making two fists, I held them up in front of me, like I was ready to box. But was I willing to fight for him? He sure didn't seem like he was fighting for me.

I walked into the dormitory and saw Raven sitting on one of the lounging chairs waiting for me. I tried not to notice what he was wearing, but I couldn't help but admire how handsome he looked wearing a short sleeve polo shirt and shorts paired with Sperry Topsiders. He smiled that oh-so-perfect greeting and my stomach released a new nest of butterflies.

"Enjoying the warm weather today?" I glanced down at his muscular legs, appraising the layers of muscles from his quads to his calves.

"When it's nice outside, I take advantage of it." He stood and my eyes traveled up his six-foot-two, two-hundred and ten pound frame. Yes, I'd checked his bio. I'd also Googled him, finding his Facebook page and a slew of articles on him.

"So, um, let's grab a room." I immediately turned away, keeping my mind focused on the task. I led him to a small study room, located to the right of the main sitting area. I closed the door behind us and we sat our stuff on the table.

"You'll be proud of me." He handed me a piece of paper.

I took it from him and glanced over it. "You already typed your blog for the week?"

"Yep," he said with a big smile as he sat across from me.

I eased into the chair and reviewed his prepared post. To my delight, he had a few paragraphs written, proving to me that he read the material beforehand. He also had very few syntax errors, which told me he had worked hard at improving his grammar. "This is great, Raven." I circled a few mistakes. "I'm so proud of you." I handed him back his paper.

His smiled faded as he studied his prepared post.

"Is something wrong?"

He shook his head. "No, I just want it to be perfect."

I leaned forward on my forearms. "And it will be. Just give yourself some time. We've only been meeting for a few weeks and look at the progress you've made."

He twitched his lips to the side. "Yeah, I guess you're right."

"So, is that it?"

He glanced at me. "Nope. I have a report due in a few weeks and I thought we could get started."

"Okay." I let out a silent sigh. I was hoping that our session would be over for the day. It was so easy to wrap myself in conversation with him that he made it hard for me to focus on Collin. And once that happened, the flirting started, the tension increased, and I found myself in situations that I knew were wrong.

"You'll be glad to know I already read the material." He handed me a book entitled, *Up From Slavery* by Booker T. Washington. The frown dissipated into one of confidence as he crossed his arms and leaned back in his chair.

"Great. Do you have the specifics about the paper?" I set the book in the middle of the table. "What the professor wants you to do? Because I doubt she wants a basic book report."

"Yep, it's all right here." He handed me the syllabus.

"Okay." I took a moment to review the instructions. "Let's start with a basic outline and incorporate the argument you'd like to make while keeping in mind the language the author uses to advance the viewpoint of the story."

"Damn, you make this sound so easy." He slumped into his chair.

Eyeing him, I said, "Don't forget I'm an English major, studying to be a teacher."

"I didn't know you wanted to be a teacher. I know you like to read, based on all the books you have on your Kindle, but I thought you might want to be a writer or something." He winked at me and the familiar rush of flutters entered my stomach.

I shrugged, trying to shake off the feeling. "Even though I love to read, I don't necessary love to write. I figured I'd be good at helping others."

He leaned forward. "And, you are."

Immediately, I broke eye contact, determined to keep to my promise and forbid my mind from thinking raucous thoughts. "Thanks. I think—"

"What the heck is all that?" Raven turned his head toward the door.

Even with the door closed, we could clearly hear a choir of voices bellowing from the main foyer. Someone played on the piano, striking keys from the lowest part of the keyboard. It made it nearly impossible to think, much less discuss his paper.

Tossing my pen on the table, I sighed. "Shit. What do you want to do?"

He stared at me intently. "We could go up to your room."

I shot a suspicious look at him. He couldn't be serious. Could he? My heart went into overdrive.

"Um, I'm pretty sure Delaney will be coming home any minute, so we won't have any peace and quiet. And the study room on my floor is always occupied by a group of foreign exchange students so that's out. We could always try the library. Oh, but you said you don't like the library." I glanced up at the ceiling, pulling anything that came to mind. "Since it's warm outside, we can head to the book store. There are tables under the awning."

Latching onto one of my wandering hands, he said, "Relax. If meeting in your room makes you uncomfortable, then we won't."

"Oh, no... it's not that." I retrieved my hand and waved off his comment, feeling like a complete idiot for rambling. I'm sure he never expected this high school behavior from a twenty-year-old woman.

"Why don't we wait until Tuesday to discuss it? I'll start thinking about my paper and try to work on the outline."

I let out a breath that apparently I had been holding. "Okay, that works. Are you sure you don't want to meet before then?"

He shoved his papers and book into his backpack. "Tomorrow night's the big game, so I'll probably be too hung-over to meet on Saturday and too tired on Sunday. Are you going to the game?"

"Um, I don't know." I cleared my throat. "I think Delaney has to do something with her family..." I spat off the first thought that came to my head because I didn't know what else to say.

Reason number thirteen: I'm becoming a liar.

"No, you have to go." He leaned across the table and I saw the determination in his gaze. "It's the biggest game of the season. And, when we're done kicking UT's ass, we're going to party our asses off. It will be one party you don't want to miss."

I threw my head back and started laughing.

"What?" He ran a hand over his head.

"Did you forget...I don't go to parties?" I reminded myself that I needed to act like *Collin Norris' fiancée.*

"Bullshit." He gave the table a friendly slap, making it shake. "I'm inviting you to this party, even if I have to pick you up myself."

"Really?" I walked out of the room and he trailed closely behind me.

"You think I'm joking, Lexi, but I swear, I'll be here in your lobby after the game, stalking you."

I laughed harder. "Don't make promises unless you're willing to keep them." I glanced over my shoulder at him.

He slapped his hands together and rubbed them viciously. "I love challenges."

Oh no. How do I get out of this one?

"Hold that thought, will you?" I pointed at him, vying for a diversion. "I have a grammar handbook I've been meaning to give you. I'll run up and get it." I started toward the elevator.

"Okay, I'll wait here."

The elevator opened and I rushed in. How had I gotten myself into that situation? I couldn't possibly go to a party with Raven. What would I tell Collin?

Thanks for taking me out to dinner and bowling, now I'm going to a party with Raven.

I unlocked the door to the suite and walked into the living room. Music played in the background and for a moment, I thought I'd left my iPod sitting on the docking station. When I saw a scarf tied around the doorknob of Delaney's room, I knew she had someone in there.

Great. Now I'll have to wait downstairs.

Scurrying to my room, I grabbed the grammar book off the shelf and another book I needed for my test next week. I shoved them into my bag and headed toward the door. Passing the coffee table, I noticed a set of familiar keys. I stopped and turned around, taking another look. A double 'S' in white lay flat on the table with several keys attached.

Keys that belonged to my brother.

I took a few steps back, covering my ears as the thoughts of Delaney and my brother having sex inundated me. My foot hit something and before I knew it, I tripped and fell back, hitting the wall. On the floor, was a large purple and grey backpack with my brother's baseball number clipped to the side.

Holy shit! They are screwing!

Not waiting a minute longer, I grabbed my bag and darted out of the dorm, slamming the door behind me. I passed the elevator and pushed through the door leading to the stairwell. I flew down the stairs and stumbled into the foyer.

"Is everything okay?" Raven extended an arm toward me, but I maintained my balance without his assistance. "Looks like you just saw a ghost."

"Worse." I gasped for air.

Raven's eye widened and he whispered, "You saw a dead body?

"What?" I took in several deep breaths, steadying my pulse.

"The only thing worse than seeing a ghost, is seeing a dead body."

He had a point, but at that moment, I couldn't think straight. I mean, how long had Delaney and Luke been hooking up? Why were they keeping it from me?

"Oh. Well, I didn't see any dead people or ghosts." I looked behind me, checking to see if they had followed me.

"Then what happened?"

With hands on my hips, I replied, "I think my roommate's screwing my brother."

With an arched brow, he leaned in closer. "Screwing as in doing him wrong or fucking him?"

"Um..." I hesitated for moment, not wanting to admit the truth. "Having sex with him." I nodded and continued to check behind me.

He chuckled. "Is that a bad thing?"

I sucked in another deep breath. "She kind of sleeps around."

"Kind of or does?"

I glanced at the floor, feeling terrible for talking about my roommate and brother to a guy who put the man in man-whore. "She does sleep around."

"If it's any conciliation, I've never slept with her." He shoved his hands in his pockets and a sly grin spread across his face.

"I can't believe you just said that." I chucked him on the arm, though I doubted my girlish thump penetrated his lumps of muscles.

"Sorry." He shrugged.

Visuals swamped my mind and everything began to spin. "Oh my God. I have to get out of here." I rushed out the door.

"Lexi, wait!" Raven called.

I rounded the building and stopped. With a hand to my forehead, I paced the area in front of me. "How could they hide something like that from me? I don't care if they are seeing each other or screwing. I just wanted to know."

"Lexi?" Raven tried to get my attention but I continued wearing down the grass.

"Did they actually think I'd never find out?"

"Lexi," Raven called one more time.

I stopped and dropped my arms beside me. "Yeah?"

"Can I take you somewhere?"

Sighing, I said, "No, that's okay. I'll be fine. I'll just, um, head to the library." I glanced around the campus, feeling off-kilter.

"Are you sure?" Raven finally caught my gaze. "Because we could hang out." He looked at his watch. "I don't have practice until three."

What? He wants to hang out with me?

"Um...well..."

"Come on," taking my hand, he towed me across the campus, "sounds like you can use a drink."

Reason number fourteen: I think I just crossed the line.

Σ

Chapter 10

I had no idea where Raven was taking me. All I knew was that we were on a university shuttle and I was in a daze. What the heck was I doing? I knew better but something propelled me to go with him. Propping my arm against the edge of the window, I watched the buildings and students zip past me. I knew from that moment forward, I couldn't take back my actions.

"You all right?" Raven leaned closer to me and his breath tingled the crevice of my neck. Every nerve woke in my body, consuming me bit by bit. My bones shuddered, but I managed to keep perfectly still. What was going on between Luke and Delaney didn't seem that important any more.

Turning toward him, I nodded.

"Don't worry, everything will be fine." He rested his arm along the back of the seat and I wanted him to be embrace me, just like he had on Sunday, when he pulled me to safety. But I knew better. I wrapped my arms around my body to self-soothe. It was the only thing I had for now.

The shuttle stopped a block from fraternity row and he got up. "Come on."

"Where are we going?" I followed him as we exited the shuttle.

"To get my car."

"Oh, okay." I resituated my bag on my shoulder and tried to keep calm. Did I really want to get in a car with him?

"Relax." He nudged me. "This will be fun."

Raising a brow, I shot him a quick look. "If you say so."

He spread his lips in to a full smile and it released some of the tension in my body. "Just wait, you'll see." We approached a white Dodge Challenger with red stripes. The lights blinked as Raven clicked the button on his key chain.

"Is this your car?" I asked as he opened the door for me.

"If it isn't then I feel sorry for the guy that it belongs to." He shut the door and then jogged around the vehicle to the driver side. He slid in and placed the key in the ignition. The engine roared to life and I hated to admit that I really liked his car. It suited him well.

"And what do you mean by that?" I clicked my seat belt over me.

"Because he missed seeing one beautiful girl in his car." He winked and pulled out of the parking lot.

I pressed my lips together, unsure of how to respond. Did he just compliment me?

You idiot, say something!

Instead, I stared at him, watching his muscles flex with every turn he took. The edge of his tattoo trailed from under the sleeve of his shirt and I refrained from reaching over and touching it. Damn, Raven was one fine specimen. As much as I didn't want to be attracted to him, it was pointless. Every hormone in my body knew his scent. Luring me in one at a time. It would take menopause to get them to stop and even then, I wasn't sure that would make a difference.

We stopped at a corner gas station. "I'll be right back." He jumped out of the car.

"Okay," I responded as the door shut.

A few minutes later he exited the store with a paper bag in hand. He opened the car door and placed the contents on the back floor board and got in the driver seat.

"What did you buy?" I stretched my neck, trying to catch a glimpse.

He shot a quick look in my direction. "You'll see."

We headed toward campus and turned on the street that led to the football stadium. I kept a close watch, anxious to know where he was taking me. Then again, I kind of liked that he didn't want to tell me. Collin rarely surprised me and the spontaneity of Raven's actions had me on the edge of my seat.

A campus security guard stationed at a small post motioned for us to stop. Raven rolled down his window and the guard leaned into the car.

"It's The Raven! What's up man?" The guard and Raven exchanged a fist bump.

"Nothing much, dude." He inclined his head in my direction. "Just gonna show her around."

"Sure thing, man." The guard patted the inside of the car with his hand. "Just make sure you have her out before practice starts." He backed away from the car.

Raven motioned with two fingers. "Will do." He drove through the entrance and across the rows of spaces, parking at the very end of the lot.

"You're taking me on a tour?" I released my seatbelt.

Before he opened his door he said, "I guess you can say that."

My heart leaped out of my chest. What the hell did he mean by that? Based on the exchange between him and the security guard, it appeared that he had brought girls there before. Was he expecting something from me?

Raven hovered in the back seat, tossing books and papers from his backpack. When it was empty, he stuffed the paper sack into it and then zipped it shut. "Let's go." He hooked the straps over his shoulders and I followed him. With every step he took the muscles in his calves bulged and my eyes traveled upward, checking out his tight butt and broad shoulders.

I sure hope he has a drink for me in that sack because I'm going to need one.

Instead of heading toward the front entrance, we sidetracked to a smaller gate. "You want us to sneak in?" I whispered, doing a quick scan to see if anyone was watching.

"Well, yeah." He pushed the gate as far as the chain would allow and I slid through effortlessly. I had never done anything so crazy before and my heart was pounding from the adrenaline that spiked my blood. I pushed on the gate, using all of my strength, and Raven squeezed his way through the narrow slit. Grabbing my hand, he led me into the stadium as he kept me tucked safely behind him.

"What happens if they catch us?" I bounced on my tiptoes, keeping a watchful eye for anyone.

Checking the main walkway, Raven said, "They'll ask us to leave."

"We won't get in trouble?"

He shrugged as we darted across the pavement to a stairwell. He pushed the door open and we scurried inside. "I hope not."

"What?" I pulled on his arm, stopping him in his tracks. "What do you mean, you hope not? I don't want to get kicked out of school." Raven unhooked his backpack and threaded my arms through it.

"Relax. They aren't going to kick you out of school. Now, get on." He squatted and motioned for me to jump on his back.

"What?" My eyes traveled up the zigzag of stairs leading to the top of the stadium. "How far are we going?"

"A couple of floors." He hit his backside as if he was a pony waiting to take his girl on a ride.

"You're going to carry me on your back," I pointed, "up several flights of stairs?"

His shoulders slumped downward. "Yes. Now, will you get on?"

I stepped closer to him and raised my leg, hesitating to climb on. Aside from horsing around with Luke when we were younger, I had never straddled a guy before, including Collin. My legs shook as they surrounded forty-five inches of muscles. Unsure of where to put my hands, I placed them on his shoulders. The swell of his blades made me want to knead them between my fingers. Inflicted with instinctive desires to touch him like I really wanted to, I focused on the top of the stairs.

"Lexi, you have to hold on tighter than that." Raven pulled my arms around his neck until the side of my face rested against his head. The scent of his cologne weakened every bone in my body, making me mold to his body's shape.

"Maybe this isn't a good idea."

He tilted his head to the side, bringing our lips mere inches apart. "Don't worry. This will be great exercise for me." With one swift movement, he laced his arms through my legs and pulled me closer, until there wasn't any space between my body and his. If I didn't die by falling, then I'd surely die of a heart attack.

"Ready?"

"I g-guess." I closed my eyes, preparing to enjoy the thrill, but my stomach and heart protested with my mind.

With speed and accuracy, Raven darted up the steps as if they were turf coated. My entire body bounced against his and I held on for dear life. "Raven, don't drop me," I squealed, as we passed one level to the next.

"I promise... I won't let you go," he said, with labored breaths. I silently wondered if what my brother had said about my ass being heavy was true. His lungs moved fiercely and I felt his heart pounding against my chest.

"If I'm too heavy, you can put me down." I eased away from him, but he gripped my legs tighter around his waist.

"Are you kidding?" he huffed. "This is nothing compared to some of the shit coach has us do." Raven continued plowing up the stairs as if he had a goal to reach. Was that goal me? Tingles spread from my head to my toes and I giggled with excitement.

"Why are you laughing?" Raven clenched onto the railing and pulled us to the next level of steps.

"This is fun!" Another roar of laughter escaped as my stomach eased and my head began to align with the vibes pouring out of every inch of my skin. I held on to him tightly, relishing in the warmth of his body against mine.

After two more flights of steps, he stopped. Sucking in a deep breath, he said, "Glad you enjoyed it." He relaxed his arms, allowing my legs to fall. "I want to show you what it's like to have a good time."

Oh, shit.

"Um... what are we going to do?" Even though my hands protested, I forced them to release the lock I had around his neck. I glided off him, straightened my shirt, and pulled up my jeans that had inched down my hips.

"You'll see," he said, turning to face me. Sweat tinged the creases in his forehead and he used the sleeve of his shirt to wipe it away. "I'll take this." His fingers grazed the top of my collarbone as he eased the backpack off my shoulders. Chills spread down my arms as I fell defenseless against his charm.

"Okay." I managed to mutter as we faced each other. Why he removed the backpack while standing in front of me, I don't know, but it was the most sensual thing I had experienced and I still had my clothes on. I couldn't even imagine what it would be like to have sex with him. Then again, I wasn't ready to do that.

He removed a badge from the outside pocket of his backpack and held it up. "I'll need this." Hooking one arm through the strap of the bag, he ushered me toward the door of the fifth floor. He scanned the badge and the door unlocked.

"This way." He led me down a hallway decorated with pictures based on the history of the previous football stadium. I ran my hand along the intricate reptile markings that lined the wall until we entered the main area.

"Wow... this is gorgeous." I did a three-sixty, taking in the ballroom filled with plush chairs and bar tables that overlooked the field. A large bronzed dragon statue, the university's mascot, stood at the front entrance. The luxurious facility showcased sleek Art Deco fixtures with a modern flair coupled with dark mahogany wood, which told me we were in the Champions Club. Luke raved about it after he went with one of his buddies to watch a game last year. If only he knew where I was — then again, it would've been devastating if he found out.

"C'mon." Raven latched onto my hand, pulling me away from the breathtaking scene and leading me up another flight of stairs. We stopped in front of a door marked, 'The Marshall's'. Using the nifty card, Raven opened the door.

"Whose suite is this?" I stepped into the lavish room that probably cost more than my college education.

"My friend, Josh." Raven closed the door and then walked to the front of the room, placing the backpack on a coffee table.

Assessing the marble bar and fifty-inch flat screen TV, I couldn't help but ask, "What does Josh do for a living?"

"Nothing yet... he's a student. This is his parents' suite." Raven removed a six pack of beer from his bag and set it on the table. A smile spread across my face. He actually remembered what I said about never drinking a beer before. If only Collin would remember things like that.

Impressive.

I sat on one of the chairs facing the window that overlooked the field. "His parents must do well to be able to pay for this space."

He chuckled and then popped the top off two beers. "His dad is in the oil and gas industry."

"Oh...with the Barnett Shell discovery here in North Texas, I'm sure his dad is fairing very well."

Raven handed me a beer. "Yes, he is."

"And they don't care if we're in here?" I took the cold bottle from his hand.

Taking a seat to the left of me, he shook his head. "Nah, sometimes we come up here with a few of the guys to drink. I thought this would be a great place to have your first beer." He tipped the edge of his bottle to mine. "Cheers."

I smiled. "Cheers." I raised the bottle to my lips and held my breath, praying it didn't taste like piss water as Luke claimed. The icy liquid slid down my throat. Surprisingly, it didn't taste as bad as I thought it would. The aftertaste was the worst, but after a few more sips, my taste buds acclimated to it.

"Should you be drinking since you have practice in," I glanced at my watch, "an hour and a half?"

He snorted. "I've played under worse conditions. Besides, we never practice that hard before a game."

"Oh, okay." I leaned closer to him. "By the way, thanks for sneaking me up here." I watched him out of the corner of my eye. "This place is really amazing."

"No problem." He propped his feet on the table and reclined in the chair. "So, do you want to talk about what's going on at your dorm?"

A picture of Luke and Delaney popped into my head and I closed my eyes as I gulped down my beer. "No, not really."

"You seemed pretty upset. Are you sure she's with your brother and not someone else?" His eyes darted to my engagement ring on my left hand. Retrieving my hand to my lap, I turned the diamond around, hiding it under the palm of my hand.

Reason number fifteen: I'm hiding the fact that I'm engaged.

"I'm pretty sure she's with my brother." I nursed the bottle, praying for a buzz to hit soon. "I saw his key chain and backpack in our living room."

Raven's cell phone rang and he pulled it from his pocket.

"Do you need to go?" I took a big gulp, reminding myself of what Delaney warned me about.

Silencing the call, he tucked the phone away. "Nope."

I tried not to react to his answer, but my mind screamed, 'yes!'

We continued drinking and Raven didn't ask me anything further about my brother and Delaney. The topic of our conversation varied between school, his dreams of going pro, and how he planned to buy his mom a new house if he did. It was the most I'd heard him talk about football since we'd met. I wanted to ask him about the rumors claiming he went to rehab for drug abuse, but I refrained. He'd tell me whenever he was ready. Besides, I had my own secrets that I wasn't ready to share either.

Raven finished his third beer and dropped it into the empty slot of the cardboard holder. Turning his head in the opposite direction, he burped.

"Nice," I said before finishing my second beer. I felt an air bubble push to the top of my stomach. I placed my hand in front of my mouth, but nothing could hide the loud belch that escaped from my lips.

"Damn, Lexi." He shot me a quick glance before turning and burping again. "I thought you said you didn't drink beer."

"Sorry," I muttered, wishing I could run out of there. "It just slipped out."

"Relax." He waved a hand. "I'm just messing with you." He handed me the last beer and I accepted it, knowing damn well that I shouldn't drink another one. But I liked the way the alcohol numbed my mind and released my worries.

"You like doing that, don't you?" I stood and walked to the wall of windows, surveying the length of the football field. I pictured Raven running across the plush grass and scoring a touchdown as the crowd cheered.

What would it take to get him to try to score one with me?

I tilted my head back and allowed the beer to fill my mouth as I swallowed. I felt him standing behind me, but I kept my body facing forward.

"Depends on what you're referring to."

My body stiffened and the phrase 'be careful what you wish for' came to mind. I picked at the label on the bottle, wishing I hadn't been thinking that way about Raven. What was wrong with me? I couldn't hurt Collin. He didn't deserve that.

I turned to walk away, but he raised his arm and leaned against the glass, trapping me. Our gazes caught and he held my conscious captive with his alluring hazel eyes.

He appraised me for a second before speaking. "If you're saying that I like to make fun of you, then you're wrong."

Holding on to my bottom lip with my teeth, I searched for the right response. "Then what would you call it?"

Taking my beer from my hand, he took a drink. "Harmless flirting."

A laugh escaped from my mouth. "Is that what Marcie...I mean, Macy would call it?"

Shaking his head, he looked down at the floor and then back at me. "No."

"No?" I asked, somewhat surprised.

He shifted his weight, causing his body to hover inches from mine. I pressed against the window as my pulse quickened. A flash of heat warmed my cheeks and I prayed he didn't notice.

"No. She's the one that flirts with me. I just play along."

I sucked in a quick breath, trying to steady my breathing. "Oh, I see. And you don't call that flirting?"

He shrugged.

"So, the rumors are all lies?"

His lips turned up and he cracked a half smile. "I didn't say that."

I narrowed my eyes at him, trying to sort through the tangled conversation in my numbing mind. "Then what are you saying? You don't have to flirt with girls because they philander with you?"

"Basically, yeah," he said, with an indifferent expression.

Great, a chauvinistic pig!

I tossed my hair over my shoulder and let the words roll off my tongue. "Then why are you flirting with me?"

"Because... I like you, Lexi Thompson." The glint in his eyes told me to stop while I was ahead but I ignored the warning.

I threw my head back and feigned a laugh. "Stop your foolish antics. You really don't like me. I mean... I'm nothing compared to the girls you've had. Usually, guys want to upgrade, not downgrade."

"Believe me," he raised a brow, "you are an upgrade."

I froze, stuck to the glass. Raven had just openly admitted that I was better than the girls he had been with.

Somebody please pinch me, I must be dreaming.

He took another swig of my beer. Condensation dripped from the bottom of the glass on to my chest. I gasped as the cold water splashed against my sizzling skin. "Sorry about that." Using the tip of his finger, he traced the trail of water leading down between my breasts.

All of the air left my lungs and my head began to spin. Never had I been touched like that. Raven was undoing me piece by piece, knitting me tighter into his trap.

I straightened and decided it was time I grow a vagina since I already had a pair of balls. I grabbed my beer from his hand and heaved a gulp. Wiping my lips with the back of my hand, I asked, "Why me?"

"Let's see, because you're not like the other girls, for one, and two, you're chaste, and that drives me crazy."

Holy shit. My vagina isn't ready for this.

The Raven was shaping and fastening me into a hot mess.

His hot mess.

"Um, okay. You know, I don't think it's a good idea for me to continue tutoring you."

His head snapped back. "Really, why?"

"Because I'm supposed to keep a professional relationship with my students and I... um... can think of fifteen other reasons why I shouldn't be helping you."

"Only fifteen?" he said in a discerning tone. In a slow, but deliberate movement, he placed his other hand against the glass, confining me between his arms.

Somebody kill me now. Please.

The air stilled around us except for our ragged breathing. My need to kiss him grew insistent, but I kept my lips under my control. Placing my hand on his chest, I pushed him away from me. "Give it time and I'm sure I'll have twenty more."

He chuckled. "Then I guess I better be on my best behavior since you're keeping count."

He laced his fingers around my wrist and dragged my hand down his chest. My hand tensed as it evaluated the rough terrain. I wanted to rip his shirt off his body and dive in, exploring every hill and valley.

Maybe my vagina is ready after all.

With my hand still glued to his stomach, I summoned the courage to respond. "If you think I'm going to let you screw me like all of those other hoes do, then you are sadly mistaken."

Lifting my hand, he drew it to his lips. His long fingers caressed my skin and I gasped.

Staring deep into my eyes he said, "Lexi, I'd never do that to you."

"Yeah, right."

"Girls like you are very rare." He placed soft kisses on the palm of my hand. The warmth of his lips fueled my deepest, inner desires, making it difficult for me to tell him to stop. Because I didn't want him to stop. Even though I knew it was wrong, I couldn't stop. He continued pressing his lips against my skin as he made a path up my arm. "You must be treated with dignity and respect."

"Are you even capable of that?" My breathing was erratic and I felt like I would pass out from lack of oxygen at any moment.

Turning my hand over, he kissed the top. "What do you think?"

"I... I don't know."

He released my hand and then cupped my face with both hands. "I guess I'll have to prove it to you."

"If you say so."

His lips lingered on the edge of mine and my alter ego begged silently for him to kiss me. "But know this, Lexi, I won't do anything, unless you ask me to do it."

A moan escaped my throat and as much as I wanted him to take me, I couldn't do it. Guilt ran through me, twisting and gnawing at my insides. I refused to cheat on Collin. He didn't deserve that.

"Raven."

He held his mouth steadily in front of mine. "Yes?"

"Take me back to my dorm, please."

Σ

Chapter 11

Raven dropped me off at my dorm without pressing me to take any further action as he promised. I thanked him for the afternoon, because it was absolutely the best time I had ever had. How many guys would take the chance to sneak you into a private owner's box in a state of the art football stadium just so you could drink your first beer? Not many. Despite how small I felt, I honestly had no regrets.

When I opened the door to our dorm, my brother's stuff was gone, leaving me to wonder if I had imagined everything.

"Delaney?" I checked around the suite, but she wasn't there. I stuck my head into her room and noticed the bedding in shambles. That was proof that what I saw two and a half hours ago, was indeed true. I shook my head, contemplating how I'd approach her and Luke about their relationship as I shut her bedroom door.

After eating a few slices of cold pizza, I took a hot shower, and sprawled on my bed with my textbooks. The words blurred on the page as I drifted off, thinking about what had happened in the stadium suite with Raven. I rolled to my back and grabbed my pillow, giggling behind it like a childish girl.

Raven confessed that he liked me.

How the hell did I end up in this situation?

Closing my eyes, I tried to come to terms with what I needed to do. The right thing was to sever the relationship with Raven and marry Collin. That's what my mom and dad would advise. But I was tired of pleasing them. I desperately needed to do what was best for me. Regardless of my decision to live my life as I wanted, I wasn't completely ready to give up on Collin. I didn't ask Raven to kiss me for a reason. I had to find out if there was any hope for my relationship with Collin.

I grabbed my phone and sent Collin a message.

Me: Thinking of you.

Holding the phone like it was my lifeline to my future, I waited patiently. Five minutes passed and there was still no response. I closed my eyes and prayed that he would answer me. After twenty minutes, I finally dropped the phone and collapsed against the mattress. *If only Collin would say something, anything, to convince me and give me the attention and love that I deserved.* He confirmed what I knew would happen.

I was giving up on him, for good.

A few hours later, my phone chimed. I rose from the bed and squinted, trying to focus on the time. I swiped the screen when I saw it was a text message from Collin.

Collin: Back from my parent's house. I'm going to take a shower and then hit the sack.

My forehead hit the pillow. Would it have killed him to come and see me?

Me: It's only 9:15.

Collin: I'm tired, Lexi.

Me: Sorry. I thought I could come over and we could watch a movie, you know like we used to. I promise, I'll be good.

It took several minutes for him to respond.

Collin: Not tonight. I really need to get some sleep. Coach scheduled a practice tomorrow afternoon since next Wednesday is the World Series game.

Of course. If I had a dollar for every excuse he made, I would've been rich.

Me: That's fine.

Collin: I already told Luke that we could go bowling tomorrow night.

I heaved a big sigh. Why didn't he tell me before Luke? Even though he lived with my brother, I deserved to be notified first. After all, I was still his fiancée.

Me: Great. I look forward to it.

Collin: I'll call you after practice so we can figure out logistics.

I considered telling him I'd like to go watch him practice, but decided against it. He tended to complain that I distracted him.

Me: Okay. Hey, have you noticed Delaney and Luke acting funny around each other?

Collin: Sort of, why?

Me: I think they hooked up earlier today.

Collin: Seriously? What makes you think that?

Me: Because I saw my brother's backpack on the floor and his keys on the coffee table.

Collin: At your dorm?

Me: Yes. Delaney's bedroom door was shut, too. I'm positive they were in there together.

Collin: He's home now.

Me: Really. Delaney was gone... My fingers hesitated because I was entering into another lie, but I couldn't tell Collin where I had been while they were screwing.

Me: when I returned home from a tutoring session.

And some session that was!

Collin: Are you going to ask her?

Me: I did the other day but she denied it. Has Luke said anything to you about her?

Collin: No and if he did, I know he wouldn't want me to say anything to you. I'd have to keep it between him and me.

What? Was he serious? Collin really wouldn't tell me if he knew something was up between my brother and Delaney? Fiancée status must've held no clout when it came to his discretion of privacy. I didn't respond, unsure of how to reply.

Collin: I'm tired. I'll call you tomorrow. Goodnight.

I stared at the screen, waiting to see if he would send me a sentiment of some sort. My finger drifted to the smiley face blowing a kiss and then pushed it. I hit the send button and waited patiently with a hopeful heart. I honestly cared for Collin. He was a good guy without any baggage or past issues. A complete contrast from Raven. Aside from placing his baseball and college studies before me, and holding on to the promise of abstinence, he really was a great catch — if he could only learn how to express his feelings toward me.

The dots on the screen faded away and it stayed fixed with my smiley face. A single tear escaped my eye and I wiped it away. Would it have killed him to tell me that he was still head over heels for me or that I had his heart? Asking for my hand in marriage didn't prove anything. Why was it so hard for Collin to show me he loved me? Then, it dawned on me.

He didn't love me.

He only liked me.

The next morning, I woke up surrounded by a few textbooks and crumbled tissues. My head throbbed and I couldn't decipher if it was from the beer or crying myself to sleep. I walked to the bathroom and did a double take when I saw how swollen my eyes were. I looked like shit and that was putting it nicely. I also felt like it.

I ran the hot water, submersing a washcloth under the faucet. I wrung the excess water and placed the steamy fabric over my face. The heat soothed my inflamed eyes and throbbing head. I opened the cabinet and took two aspirins.

My phone chimed and I walked back to my room. I searched the covers, finally locating the phone near the foot of my bed. The time flashed, five after twelve.

"Crap!" I had missed all my classes. I dropped to the bed, wondering how the heck I slept through my alarm. I checked my phone and realized that I hadn't turned it on.

Oh well.

I switched to my text messages and saw that I had a few from Delaney and one from Raven. My heart immediately went into overdrive.

Pressing on Raven's message, the date stamp showed ten forty-four last night.

*Raven: Had a great time today. Can't wait to have more fun with you. *wink.*

I smiled and within seconds, the pain in my head ebbed but the one in my heart increased. Resting the phone to my chin, I wondered if I should respond. Without further thought, I typed a message.

Me: Me too.

Not waiting for a response, I scrolled to Delaney's text.

Delaney: Hey, I'm staying with Jordan tonight. I'll be back tomorrow after class.

Yeah, right. She was with my brother. I just knew it.

That message was followed with another one.

Delaney: Hey, we're planning to leave at six tonight to go eat Sushi on 7th Street and then to the bowling alley after that. What did Collin say?

What? As if she didn't already know. I shook my head.

Me: He said we could go.

A few seconds later, she replied:

Delaney: Finally! Did you just wake from the dead?

Me: Yeah, basically. Missed class, too.

Delaney: Shame on you. Anyhow, I'll be there within the hour. Want anything to eat? I'm at the deli.

I wanted to be mad at her, but she seemed so happy. I couldn't stay angry, so I shoved it off.

Me: Sure. I'll take a grilled chicken salad with Italian dressing, please.

Delaney: You got it.

I grabbed the remote and turned on the TV, not feeling up to getting dressed or studying. Flipping through the channels, I landed on some reality cooking show and watched the contestants go crazy as they tried to finish their dish within the allotted time.

Thirty minutes later, the front door to our suite opened and Delaney walked in.

"Hey, got your salad." She held up a plastic sack as she fumbled to pull the key from the lock.

"Thanks." I rose from the couch to help her.

She tossed her overnight bag and backpack in the doorway to her room. "You look like crap. What happened to you?"

I shrugged. "Nothing... just Collin issues." I wanted to tell her what happened at the stadium yesterday with Raven but decided against it.

She winced. "I thought you said he wanted to hang out tonight."

Opening the sack, I pulled out my salad and drizzled the dressing over it. "He does."

"Then, what's the problem?"

"Same crap as last week." I stabbed the lettuce with a fork and took a bite.

Delaney sighed. "I'm sorry." She plopped down next to me on the sofa and pressed against me. "Everything will be all right." The smell of my brother's cologne wafted from her hair and I debated over asking her about yesterday afternoon. Instead, I blew it off and forced myself to eat.

"We're going to have a great time tonight," she said, in a sing-song voice.

"You might, I doubt I will." I picked at the vegetables in my salad, becoming fuller by the second.

"Come on." She shook me. "Don't think that way. Just relax, be yourself, and have a good time with Collin."

I leaned to the side so I could get a better look at her. "Are you drunk?"

She burst into laughter. "No!" Darting up from the couch and over to her bag, she pulled out a big white bottle and showed it to me. "But I will be by tonight."

I swallowed and then took a sip of water from the bottle left on the coffee table. "What's that? Looks tropical."

"This, my dear, is Malibu's finest." She held the bottle as if she were a sales model on an infomercial. "The original Caribbean Coconut Rum with a refreshing blend of white rum with coconut. It's a taste of paradise you can enjoy anytime!" Her voice lilted as she read the back label.

Laughing, I got up and took the bottle from her. I unscrewed the cap and took a whiff. "Smells good. How does it taste?"

"Like someone just came in your mouth," she smiled.

"Gross." I screwed the cap back on, trying to displace the thought of my brother's semen in her mouth.

She giggled. "Sorry, but it does taste really good mixed with Coke."

My eyes swept over the bottle before handing it back to her. "Maybe I'll try it."

"That's my girl." She held her hand up in the air and I gave her a high five. "Okay, but before we get our party started, I desperately need to take a nap." She trailed off toward her room, shaking her butt.

"Why? Didn't get any sleep last night?" I pried, waiting to see how she'd respond.

"No, we stayed up late watching movies and then I got up early to go to class," she yelled from the bathroom. The shower turned on and the door shut. How long would she keep up this charade? I huffed out a breath, trying to blow the strands of hair hanging in my face. Then, I got up and tossed my salad in the trash. I'd confront them tonight.

Σ

Chapter 12

A few hours later, we were dressed and waiting downstairs for Collin and Luke to pick us up. Since Jordan lived off campus in an apartment with two other girls, Delaney told them we'd meet them at the restaurant.

"How do I look?" Delaney adjusted her top, making her boobs bounce, and then pulled up on her skinny jeans.

"Like you're ready to go hoeing around," I said, matter-of-fact.

Delaney gasped and then covered her chest. "Do I really?"

"I'm just messing with you," I snickered. "Honestly, you look fine. Pretty, actually."

She sighed. "You scared me for a minute." Her face brightened. "Which reminds me..." she darted toward the elevators.

"Where are you going?"

"Forgot something!" She dashed through the elevator doors.

I turned and saw Collin walking into the front foyer.

A smile formed across both our faces and I waved.

"Hi." He leaned forward and pressed his lips to my cheek. "You look pretty."

"Thank you and you look handsome." I took in his pressed, plaid button-down shirt and starched jeans. His sandy-blond hair swept to the side and his green eyes sparkled. Collin had the picture perfect face of an all-American boy.

But did I belong with him in that picture?

"Thank you." He inclined his head and I saw a faint flash of pink across his clean-shaven face. "Are you ready?"

"Yes." I looked over my shoulder. "Delaney can meet us in the car."

He held out his elbow and I wrapped my hand around his arm. It was nice to be close to him but I knew that was the closest our bodies would ever be, at least while we were unwed. I tried to focus on the positives and give Collin the chance that he deserved. That we deserved. Despite what my gut told me, I knew that if I didn't at least try, I'd hate myself for it. We walked to Luke's Camaro and as usual, he opened the door for me. I slid in the back.

"Hey, Brother."

"Sis." Luke barely glanced at me and I sensed he wasn't in a good mood.

Instead of Collin sitting in the front with Luke as he normally did, he sat in the back with me. My heart fluttered and I couldn't help but smile when he took my hand and laced his fingers through my mine. It seemed like ages since we last held hands or sat that close together.

A few minutes later, the car door opened and Delaney got in. "Sorry," she huffed as she struggle to pull the door shut, "had to get something."

"Do you have everything?" Luke kept his hand steady on the gearshift.

"Um, let me check." She dug around in her purse.

Luke sighed and Collin and I traded glances with one another but didn't say anything.

"Yep. I'm good."

He shifted the car into drive. "I hope so because I'm not coming back." He gave her a quick once over and then turned his head to face forward.

I swore they sounded like two old married people. Raking my mind, I tried to recall the first time I saw them interacting on a more than friendly manner. I gave up when Luke cranked up his stereo. I started humming to the beat of the music.

Thoughts of rubbing Collin's leg crossed my mind, but after recalling what happened last time, I decided to keep my hands to myself. Regardless of keeping my actions under control, my body had a mind of its own, begging for him to touch me. I knew it would never happen unless I married him, and even then, I wasn't sure he would indulge.

We parked in the parking garage and walked toward the restaurant. Strings of white lights hung between the buildings, energizing the swanky hangout as people darted in and out of restaurants, bars, and shops. Everywhere I looked, I saw happy couples, holding hands, kissing, and cuddling.

I wanted that.

I needed that.

I didn't have that.

The cool evening air swept through the trees and I stretched my sweater over me. Providing myself with that comfort that I wished he would give me.

"Are you cold?" Collin asked, sliding an arm around me.

I flinched, not prepared to feel his warm embrace. Did he finally recognize my need for affection? Had that talk resonated within him? "Yeah, a little."

He wrapped his arm around me and I snuggled closer to him, wedging myself under his chin. We entered the Sushi café and squeezed our way through the crowd.

"Luke, Collin..." Forbes raised a finger, calling our attention as we entered.

"Glad you guys got us a table." Luke gave Forbes a pat on the back.

Forbes placed an arm behind his girlfriend, Jordan. "Us, too. As soon as we were seated, the place filled up."

Collin shook hands with Forbes. "Where's Matt?"

"He and Ali decided to do something else," Forbes replied.

"Oh, too bad." Displaying his perfect manners, Collin pulled out a chair for me before sitting down. I sat next to Jordan. Luke and Delaney sat across from us and a little too close for two people who were supposedly only friends.

"Hey, Lexi, love your hair." Jordan latched on to a lock of my waves.

"Thanks, love yours, too." Her golden hair was swept to the side with several braids intertwining throughout. "I wish I could braid my own hair."

"I've been doing it forever." Jordan fiddled with a few strands. "Anytime you want me to braid your hair, just let me know."

"Okay, I will." I turned when I heard my brother and roommate chat about whether to get separate entrees or share a few rolls. Apparently, they had been there before. Together. My impatience grew and I was eager to confront them. I don't know why I had to know the truth. Maybe a part of me felt a little jealous that Luke had done what our parents told him not to do. Yet, I was the one engaged and hadn't experienced half the stuff he had.

After everyone agreed to order the 'Titanic' boat, filled with several pieces of sushi, rolls, and sashimi, we talked and laughed about school, tests, and the upcoming baseball game. Every fall, PHU held a purple and white game, closing out the fall practice season. The team played against each other in a three series game that started on Wednesday and ended on Sunday afternoon.

Once we finished off the huge assortment of rolls, we walked to the bowling alley. To my disappointment, Collin stayed a few steps ahead of me, not bothering to hold my hand. Even though it was only one block from the restaurant, it still hurt. We rode the elevator to the second floor and when the doors opened, dance music blared through the speakers. On one side of the building was a large bar with pool tables and a small dance floor. To the right were the bowling lanes. Neon lights colored the dim establishment and plush sofas and chairs lined the walls.

I took my check card out of my purse. "Hey, I'll pay for us since you paid for dinner."

A look of confusion twisted across Collin's face. "Thanks for offering, but I've got it."

"Are you sure?"

"Yes." He pushed my hand away.

I dropped the card into my purse. "I thought maybe I should start offering to pay."

He removed a couple of bills from his wallet and then turned to me. "In the four years we've been together, I've never expected you to pay for us. I don't expect for you to start now."

I looked at him through narrowed eyes, unsure if he was being nice or controlling. Other girls might have been thrilled to hear that, but it didn't set well with me. If it would have been Raven, that would've been a different story. Before I could say anything, he leaned forward and kissed me on the forehead.

"Size seven, right?" Collin handed Luke his money as he and Forbes worked out the details for renting the lanes.

"Yes," I replied.

"She needs a seven and I need an eleven," Collin informed the girl behind the counter.

She handed us our bowling shoes. "I've set up lane one for you guys."

"Thanks," I said, taking them from her.

"Come on, let's go." Delaney grabbed her shoes and motioned for us to follow her.

"I want to go first." Delaney typed her name into the scoring console, followed by Luke's.

"We can go last," Collin offered as he sat down to change his shoes.

"Okay." Delaney shrugged. "I guess that means you and Forbes are in the middle," she told Jordan.

"That's fine." Jordan tugged, trying to pull off her boots.

"Here, doll, let me help you." Forbes rushed to her side. He gave a quick tug and slipped off her boot. Then, he picked up her other leg, and did the same. Before setting her foot down, he kissed the top of it.

"Stop, pumpkin." Jordan giggled as he trailed kisses up her calf.

"Hey," Luke walked through the aisle, cutting in between them, "there'll be none of that tonight."

Forbes gave Luke a playful push. "Get out of here, man."

Luke sidestepped, breaking a fall, and then looked around at the TV's hanging on the walls. "The game is starting. I'll ask if they can turn it on." He jogged to the front desk.

The TV to the left of us switched from a hockey game to the football game. Immediately, Raven's picture flashed on the screen and my heart skipped a beat. The sports newscasters were speaking but since the volume was on mute, I had no idea what they were saying. My brother and Forbes discussed the game and whom they thought would score more points. They also debated on how Raven would do if he had his shit together.

"Lexi," Collin interrupted my drooling, "let's find you a ball."

I walked to the return ramp and picked up a ten-pound ball.

"That's too heavy." He shook his head. "You can hurt your wrist. I think you should try something lighter."

"Okay," I said, setting the ball down. Since I hadn't bowled in a few years, I trusted Collin's advice.

He handed me a purple and pink swirled ball. "Try this one."

"Seven pounds?" I took the ball from him. "Looks like a kid's ball."

"That's because it is," Delaney teased as she sunk her fingers into a nine-pound ball and then walked up to the lane.

"Just try it," Collin urged.

"Don't listen to her." Jordan leaned over my shoulder. "I use a seven-pound ball too."

I smiled at her. "Great. We can share this one." I placed the ball on the rack and then turned my attention to the TV.

"Strike!" Delaney yelled.

"Yeah, baby!" Luke gave her a high-five and then popped her on the butt. Delaney jumped and then laughed it off.

Just friends. Yeah, right.

I turned in time to see the receiver miss the catch. "Aw, man." I stomped my foot on the ground.

"Damn." Forbes stood next to me, watching the game.

"Since when did you care about football?" Delaney elbowed me as she shuffled past me. I gave her a warning stare and then sat next to Collin. I had never taken a keen interest in football since I spent most of my time on the baseball fields with Luke and Collin. Meeting Raven had piqued my interest mainly because I wanted to see him play.

"What are you doing?" I leaned against Collin, trying to catch a glimpse of his phone.

He kept his eyes trained on the screen. "Checking the baseball scores." Abruptly, he stood up and looked around. "The Rangers are playing."

"Ten in the pit!" Luke yelled and Delaney exchanged a fist bump with him. "Your turn, Lexi."

"Show off," I muttered as I walked to the ramp and jammed my fingers into the slots. Bearing the heavy ball, I stood in front of the line, extended my arm back, and then dumped it on the lane. It rolled down the wood to the right and immediately went into the gutter.

"Darn!" I turned around, mad that it didn't make it half way down.

"Stand back and then walk into the roll," Jordan explained, trying to show me how to do it.

"It's okay, Jordan. I suck at sports." I gave her a kind smile.

"Show her, pumpkin." Jordan pulled on Forbes arm, trying to coax him into helping me.

Forbes waved off Jordan. "Hey, Collin."

Collin stood behind our seating area, facing the wall that displayed the baseball game. "Yeah?"

"Show your girl how to hook a ball."

Looking over his shoulder, Collin spotted me.

"Please?" I clutched the cement ball with both hands.

Collin's shoulders slumped and he lumbered toward me. He didn't want to help me. I was disturbing his baseball game, even though we were out on a date. A date he promised when he failed to spend time with me. Nothing had changed. The sweetness and politeness were overcome by his true love.

Baseball.

"Did you forget how to bowl?" He eased the ball from my hands, but I saw the discontent in the depths of his eyes.

"Yes, it's been a while."

He gave me a slight smile and then slid his fingers in the holes and approached the lane. "Stand back a few feet," he demonstrated while I watched carefully, "and then walk up to the foul line, but be careful not to cross it. Swing your arm back, and then release it with a flick of your wrist."

The ball shot down the alley with speed, crashing into the pins and knocking every one of them down.

"Strike!" I clapped as Collin walked past me. "You make it seem so easy." I trailed behind him, dying for some attention.

"That's because it is easy."

"For you," I added.

He turned around with a twelve-pound ball in hand. "All you have to do is try."

"I am. But I can't help it if I don't have any coordination." I stepped aside and watched him throw the ball with ease and precision as if it were a baseball, earning another strike. Luke and Collin were just alike. Skilled at almost any sport they played. I wondered how he would fare on the football field. Although he was built like a lean running machine, at five-foot-eleven and one-hundred and eighty pounds, he was smaller than Raven and most football players. That's why baseball suited him.

"Way to go!" I threw my arms around him, but he stayed as stiff as a board, keeping the wall up between us. After a few awkward seconds, I let go.

"Excuse me." Collin flagged the waitress. "Can you bring us a few drinks?"

"Sure." The petite girl with blonde and pink striped hair took our order and then jotted down Luke's and Forbes'.

I sat on the sectional, facing the TV and tugged on Collin's hand. "Sit next to me."

"Okay." He eased to the plush sofa but swiveled around, facing the back TV to watch the Rangers play. I crossed my arms and sighed, keeping one eye on the TV and the other on my friends. Once again, I was all alone.

After Jordan and Forbes bowled, Delaney walked up to the return ramp. With her butt aimed at Luke, she leaned over and huffed as she tried to reach her bowling ball. "Hey, Luke, do you think nine-pounds is too light? Would I do better with a ten-pound ball?"

Luke watched her pensively before getting up to help her. I elbowed Collin and motioned for him to watch, but he rolled his eyes and returned his focus to the TV screen.

"Just keep using the nine-pound one." He winked at her. "You're doing great."

I wanted to say, 'busted', but when I saw the way my brother looked at her, I let it go. Since we were all adults, they could do whatever the hell they wanted. It still hurt that neither of them felt like they could confide in me. And I wanted to know why.

Several turns later, Delaney grabbed me just as I was about to set my soda on the table. "Come with me to the bathroom."

"Oh, okay."

"And bring your drink," she whispered in my ear as she swung her purse over her shoulder.

I thought about telling Collin I'd be right back, but he was glued to the game. I followed her to the bathroom and she pulled me into the handicap stall with her.

Before I could say anything, she handed me her drink. "Here, hold this." Then, she reached into her purse, pulling out a plastic flask.

"Did you bring that from home?"

She nodded. "That's why I had to go back upstairs. I almost forgot it."

Based on Luke's comment, I wondered if he asked her to bring it. The fruity smell filled the small space and it called to me, tempting me to drown myself in the cool liquid that would take away all my hurt. Then, I thought about what happened last Sunday. "That's okay, I better not." I pulled my drink away from her.

"Oh, come on," she hounded. "Just one drink."

"No, Collin will get mad."

She glanced at me through her thick lashes. "I see how miserable you are...sitting all by yourself while he watches the baseball game."

"I know," I sighed. "But he wants to see it."

"Well, let him watch it." She tossed her long waves over her shoulder. "I doubt he'll notice. Besides, you deserve to have a good time tonight."

She had a point, I did deserve to have a good time, but drinking in front of Collin would be disastrous. "You're wrong. He'll smell the liquor and when he does, he'll be pissed. I better not."

"Suit yourself." Delaney poured two capfuls of the sweet rum into her soda.

"Dang, Delaney. Isn't that too much?"

"Nah." She mixed the drink with a red straw and then tasted it. "Wow, it is a little strong but perfect for Luke."

"Really?" Had she and Luke drank together? She made it seem like it was a regular thing for him. I watched as she tightened the cap on the flask, tossed it into her purse, and then zipped it closed.

"Delaney, I need to ask—"

"Let me in." Jordan knocked on the bathroom door.

I opened the door and Jordan scurried in, soda in hand. "Let me guess, you need your drink flavored, too?"

"You bet, girl." Jordan took a gulp of her soda before holding it out for Delaney to spike.

"What about Forbes?" Delaney asked.

Jordan took a quick taste. "He got a beer."

"Oh, that's right, he's twenty-one."

We scurried out of the bathroom and returned to our seats. Luke had a beer in hand along with Forbes. Apparently, Forbes had bought it for him since Luke wasn't of age and Collin wasn't twenty-one either. As usual, Collin sipped on his water with lemon.

"I guess I'll be drinking this one." Delaney lifted the glass intended for Luke and took a drink. Her mouth and eyes twisted like she had swallowed hot coffee.

"A little strong?" Luke joked.

"Yeah, I made it for you." Delaney licked her lips and I rolled my eyes.

"Wanna trade?" Luke lifted up his bottle of beer.

Delaney shook her head. "Um, no thanks."

Forty-five minutes and several drinks later, my friends were laughing and having a good time. Collin watched the baseball game the entire night, only getting up when it was his turn to bowl. Every now and then, he'd say something to me. I kept a watchful eye on the football game, cheering every time we scored. Garnering bravery, I slipped my cell phone from my pocket and texted Raven a message of good luck. Even though I knew he wouldn't see it until after the game was over, I wanted him to know I was thinking about him.

"Get off your phone and hurry up!" Luke tried to take Delaney's phone away, but she jerked her hand away from him. "We only have a few minutes left."

"Okay, okay. I was just posting some pics of us." She shoved her phone into her back pocket and stumbled toward the return rack. She turned around with Luke's twelve-pound ball.

"She's gonna do it!" Jordan cheered and then pulled me to get up to watch her.

"Don't fall!" I warned her as she giggled.

"I won't." She waved her hand and nearly lost her balance. "Whoa." She turned around and gave us a thumbs up.

She tossed the ball and it wobbled down the wood, veering to the left and then straightening as it hit the center.

"I almost got a strike!" Delaney danced around.

"That's great. Now quit jacking around," Luke scolded. "You still have another turn. Let's see if we can all roll before the time is up."

"All right. All right," she barked.

She retrieved the heavy ball and scurried to the lane. Taking several steps back, she positioned herself, clutching the ball to her chest as she eyed her prize.

One standing pin.

Delaney swung her arm back, took a few steps forward, and went airborne. The twelve pounder flew from her hand as her feet slipped against the slick floor. Her body crashed to the floor as she landed on her butt.

Jordan leaped forward. "Laney!"

"Oh, shit!" Luke's voice echoed in the background.

"Oh my God!" I screamed, sliding across the floor on my knees. "Are you okay?"

Luke and Forbes helped her sit up. "Did you hurt yourself?" Luke checked her head, arms, and then her legs.

She rubbed her backside. "I busted my ass, that's all."

"What the heck happened?" Collin hovered behind me. "Delaney slipped and fell."

"Better slow down on the drinks, missy," Forbes teased as he patted her back.

Collin humphed and then walked off.

With one hand behind her back and the other around her hand, Luke helped Delaney stand.

"Oh man!" Delaney cried as she pulled her phone from her back pocket. "My screen shattered."

"Damn, that's the second phone you've had this year," Luke complained.

"Well if you wouldn't have been rushing me, then this wouldn't have happened!" Delaney yelled.

Luke took a step back. "Don't blame it on me. You're the one that had too much to drink."

With her hands on her hips, Delaney eyed Luke. "I'm not—"

"I think you dropped your ball." Riley Stokes, one of the guys on the baseball team walked up to Luke and shoved it into his chest.

Luke grunted, but kept a straight face. "Whatever." They stared at each other for a few seconds before Luke placed the ball on the return ramp. He fisted his hands but kept them at his sides. Luke usually didn't get in to fights with guys, but for whatever reason, he and Riley didn't get along.

Riley smirked, then turned around and started to walk off. He stopped and looked at Delaney. "Next time, you might want to help your boyfriend find his ball." He covered his mouth, trying to hide his snickering.

"Screw you, Riley," Delaney snapped.

Riley's eyes swept over her and then a grin spread across his face. "We already did, remember?"

"Asshole!" Luke leaped over the ball return ramp and grabbed a fistful of Riley's shirt, spinning him around. Luke swung, landing a punch in the center of Riley's face. Riley bowed, surprised from the attack, but came back at Luke, throwing a left hook. Luke blocked Riley's arm and then swung again, this time hitting him in the stomach.

"Stop!" Delaney yelled.

Collin and Forbes rushed to pull Luke off Riley. "Come on, guys!" Forbes yelled, trying to stop Luke from throwing punches.

"Coach is going to be mad," Collin reminded Luke and Riley as he tried to separate the two.

Another baseball player, Winston, latched on to Riley's arms. "I'll whip both your asses if you don't stop!"

The six-foot-three player picked up Riley like a rag doll. Riley flung his legs and landed a kick on the edge of Luke's chin, whipping his head to the side. Luke stumbled back, nearly crashing into Delaney as he grasped his face. Delaney crouched down next to him. "Luke, are you okay?"

"I'm good." Luke shoved away from Delaney.

"Get off me, Winston, I'm warning you!" Riley yelled as his feet thrashed about, kicking anything that got in his way. Collin ducked, but staggered back as Riley's foot missed him by mere inches. I rushed to his side, making sure he was okay.

"Everyone, out of here now!" Two security guards dressed in black from the front door yelled at us.

"We need to go, now." Forbes rushed past us with Jordan in tow.

Luke took Delaney by the hand as they both kicked off the bowling shoes and grabbed their own shoes. He motioned for us to follow him out the door.

Collin and I quickly changed our shoes, leaving our bowling shoes with everyone else's. "Here's your purse and coat." Collin handed me my stuff and then shuffled us down the stairs. I looked behind us to see Winston and Riley arguing with the guards. The front door flew open and we bolted out on to the sidewalk. That night had officially gone to shit.

Σ

Chapter 13

The weekend flashed by and I found myself getting ready to go to the World Series game. Somehow, I had managed to get through the meetings with the photographers, church, and lunch, sans the Mimosas. Even though I had needed one badly. Seeing pictures of couples displaying their blissfulness had pointed out one thing: Collin and I didn't have that level of happiness. When I looked at us, I didn't see a spark or glow coming from our faces, especially not mine. There was something missing in our picture.

Love.

It made me more confident in my decision to not marry him. Delaney was right. Our relationship existed on a friendship level and we were only marrying out of expectancy. I wished Collin would've seen that so it would've been a mutual break up. I could only hope that once I mentioned it, he would agree. One thing was certain though, I was telling him after the game.

The door to our suite opened and I heard Delaney humming. I'd managed to ignore her for the past several days, but I knew I couldn't keep doing that. I really needed to talk to her about my decision.

"Lexi?" Delaney knocked on the door as I slipped on my boots.

"Yeah, come in."

She partially opened the door and stood in the doorway, hesitant to enter.

"Are you going to the game?"

I really didn't want to go, but since our parents were coming to watch the game, I knew that would be a bad move on my part.

They'd wonder why I wasn't going and I didn't feel like explaining myself to them.

"What do you think?" I held out my arms, showing her my purple sweater, which supported Collin's team.

With a slight smile, she opened the door further, showing me her white ruffled shirt. "I'm going too."

"Supporting Luke?" I asked, already knowing the answer.

She wrapped her arms around her body and stared at the floor. I had never seen Delaney hang her head in shame. Maybe the guilt had finally gotten to her.

"It's okay, Delaney. You can quit pretending now." I approached her and moved the hair dangling in front of her face to over her shoulder. "I know you and Luke have been seeing each other."

She looked at me with eyes that begged for forgiveness and there was no way I could hold on to the deceit. "Are you mad?"

"No." I shook my head. "Just disappointed that you didn't tell me."

"I'm sorry." She let out a big sigh. "I wanted to, but Luke thought it was best if we just kept it between us."

"Why? I don't understand."

"It's complicated." Her eyes traveled to the floor and then back up at me. "We're not together, together..."

I sat down. In a weird, girlie way, I kind of understood why she didn't tell me. She probably didn't want me to get upset since it was my brother she was messing around with and not just another one of her 'pick of the day' guys. It had taken a lot of nerve for me to tell her about Raven and she didn't even know him.

It's definitely harder when you know the person.

"So you're more like friends with benefits?"

"Yeah," she shrugged. "I guess you can say that."

"I know you're not the type that sticks with one guy, but all I ask is that you treat Luke right and not hurt him.

"I like Luke, I really do." She collapsed on the bed, next to me. "I'm just not ready to settle down, not yet." She stared at me, waiting for me to say something.

"Don't look to me for advice." I shot her a quick glance. "I can't even find the nerve to tell Collin I don't want to marry him."

She stayed silent for a moment and then said, "So you're one-hundred percent sure that's what you want?"

My throat tightened and my eyes watered. I pressed my lips together and nodded. Despite wanting that, it didn't make it any easier. Delaney wrapped her arm around me and I closed my eyes. Tears streamed down my cheeks and I wiped them away. "I can't get through to him. No matter what I do or say, he won't change. It's like he's wearing a shield that protects his emotions and a vice that surrounds his heart. Apparently I don't have the power to penetrate that combination lock."

"Some guys just don't get it." She shook her head.

"Sad, but true." I glanced at her through wet lashes. "I know now that our relationship exists on a friendship level. I can't marry him knowing that we aren't madly in love with one another."

"And you're not doing this in hopes of being with Raven?"

"Seriously?" I pushed away from her. "You really think I'm leaving Collin to be with Raven?"

She recoiled against the wall and then wrapped her arms around her legs. "I don't know. I mean you've told me the way you feel about him and I've seen it with my own eyes."

Delaney was right. I was attracted to Raven and I really did enjoy being around him. He had brought out a part of me that I didn't even know existed. When I was with him, I had a fire that burned bright inside of me, making me feel alive to the point he moved me like no one else could. I had had to keep that fire contained, so that I knew I was making the right decision to not marry Collin. Even though a part of me wanted to run back to him and let him light that fire once again.

"Look, I might like him, but I promise you, I'm not doing this so I can be with him."

"Okay. I believe you."

I relaxed and leaned against the wall, next to her. "I even canceled my session with him yesterday. And I'm not sure I'll continue tutoring him." Not to mention, I had refused to respond to his text messages on Friday night when he said he was downstairs waiting to take me to the party. That was the hardest thing I had ever done. Knowing that all I had to do was go six floors down and let him show me the time of my life.

She leaned her head against mine. "Then you're doing the right thing and shouldn't feel guilty. It'll be hard, but in the end, you'll be glad you did this."

"I hope you're right."

"Me, too." Silence filled the space between us and then she said, "When are you going to tell him?"

"Tonight, after the game." I checked my phone. Every minute seemed to pass in thirty second increments, bringing me closer to what I had to do. "I can't keep going on like this. I'm miserable."

"I know. I'm here for you," she squeezed my hand, "no matter what."

Relief settled the nausea in my stomach and the fear entwined in my mind. "Thanks, Delaney. I appreciate that."

A few minutes later, my phone rang. I glanced at the screen before answering it. "Crap, it's my mom."

"Hello?"

"Hey, Lexi, we're down the street. Do you need a ride to the stadium?"

"Yeah, sure. Can you give Delaney a ride, too?"

"Of course. See you in a minute."

I hung up the phone. "My parents are picking us up in a few minutes."

"Okay, good." Delaney got up and then pulled me to my feet. "C'mon. You can do this."

I took a deep breath and let it out. "If you say so."

We put on our jackets and headed downstairs to my parents' car.

"Hi, girls. How's your week so far?" Mom turned around, giving us a quick glance.

Horrible. I shrugged, not responding.

"Busy," Delaney replied and clicked her seat belt.

"Good to see you both." Dad smiled through the rearview mirror. I managed to smile back.

"I have good news, Lexi." Mom's voice lilted and I cringed.

"What's that?"

"I was able to schedule an appointment with the photographer the Gilford's recommended for next Saturday."

"Great," I said, not caring if I sounded disappointed. Mom had asked one of the couples that joined us for lunch on Sunday about their daughter's photographer. She had recently married and mom had quickly become engrossed with the details of their wedding. I had played along, once again, acting like I cared when I really didn't.

Mom turned around. "What's wrong?"

I quickly averted my eyes and stared out the window. "Nothing."

"Are you sure? You sound a little down."

"I'm fine." Riding in the car with them was more trouble than it was worth. Walking in the cool temperatures would have been better than the interrogation.

"Well, I wasn't going to tell you this, but what the heck." My head snapped in her direction.

Oh, please don't tell me anything else about the wedding!

"Your dad and I went to the bridal shop and guess what?"

My stomach did a somersault and I had to hold the vomit threatening to purge from me.

She continued, even though I didn't respond. "We bought you that wedding dress!" She clapped her hands and I wanted to jump out of the car into incoming traffic.

"The one she didn't like?" Delaney blurted.

Could my life get any worse?

"What?" Mom sounded surprised by Delaney's response. "That dress is perfect."

"The dress is really pretty, Lexi," Dad spoke up. "Is there a reason you didn't like it?" I was shocked that Mom allowed him to have input about the wedding and what she wanted me to wear.

"If you like being covered up to your neck in lace," I huffed.

Delaney motioned for me to stay calm. I had to bite my tongue before I announced that the wedding was off. I took a deep breath and prayed for strength.

"Mom showed me the other dress—"

"The strapless one?" Dad's comment quickly caught my attention.

"Yes." His voice thickened and I slumped in my chair. "That wasn't appropriate and you know it."

Please kill me now, because I can't take one more minute of this shit!

I don't know why I let it bother me since I wasn't planning on getting married, but it did. Maybe it was because reality had hit. After that night, I wouldn't be Collin's fiancée. He'd never see me wearing that wedding dress, even though it was ugly as hell. Or maybe it was another reminder of how my parents controlled my life. My head and my heart were a convoluted mess of emotions.

The car stopped and I opened the door, gasping for air. I couldn't breathe and the weight of the stress was consuming my body. I darted across the grass parking lot and headed toward the stadium, even though that was the last place I wanted to go.

"Lexi, what's the problem?" Dad yelled, following me.

With a sigh, I stopped. "Nothing. Just forget about it." I tracked in a circle, holding on to my head as I prayed for God to make me an emotionless person like Collin. It would have been so much easier to not feel the hurt and lack of love that I needed.

"Why are you so upset? What's going on?" Mom's hounding raked over my skin.

Delaney stood behind them, instructing me to stay quiet. She was right. I had to tell Collin before I told my parents. It wouldn't be fair to him.

"I've had a rough week and the wedding is stressing me out." I crossed my arms and shuffled my feet. "Can we please not talk about it anymore tonight?"

"Okay. Just calm down." Dad slipped his arm around me and I leaned into him, feeling some of the stress melt away. "We won't say another word." He turned and gave Mom his typical pleading eyes stare. I doubted she'd do as he said, since she always got her way.

With Dad's arm firmly wrapped around me, we walked to the stadium. It took all of my effort to keep the waterworks from releasing. I really wanted to confide in him and tell him what was going on in my life, but I knew he would side with my mom. He'd tell me I was being irrational; that the stress was getting to me and I'd regret my decision. I knew what I had to do, though. I was only waiting for the right time.

We headed to the usual pizza place the baseball team went to after the game. The smell of dough wafted through the air. Normally my stomach would have welcomed several slices of their house special stacked with Applewood smoked bacon, but food was the last thing I wanted. Delaney, Jordan, and I sat in an oversized booth while my parents gathered with Collin's family.

"Way to go!" Several people chanted and whistled as a few baseball players wearing purple entered the restaurant. Cheers continued to follow as more of the team filed in. I kept a watchful eye, waiting for Collin to enter.

Riley and Winston walked in and Delaney shifted in her seat. "Great. Why did they have to come?" They immediately spotted us and headed in our direction.

"Just ignore them." I rolled my eyes at Riley when his stare turned annoyingly smug. They passed our booth and sat at a table with some other players near the back.

"Don't worry." Jordan patted Delaney on the hand. "Surely they aren't stupid enough to try something with everyone here."

Delaney whimpered, "It's not them I'm worried about."

"My parents are here," I reminded her. "I'm sure Luke will be on his best behavior... or should be."

"I hope so," Delaney sighed when she saw Luke walk through the door.

"Woot! Woot! Go, Collin! Go, Collin!" The purple team cheered when Collin stepped into the restaurant. Forbes trailed behind them, shouting along the way, "MVP. MVP." He pointed to Collin and I couldn't help but smile.

Collin had pitched a near perfect game, sweeping the white team twelve to one. He never ceased to amaze me with his precision and gift for playing baseball. Every year he seemed to get better and better. Even though I hated that he put baseball before me, I was a little sad knowing that I would no longer be there to cheer him along. Despite my decision not to marry him, I hoped we could remain friends. I'd watched him play since we were thirteen years old and we'd practically grown up together. He really was a great guy, just not the right one for me.

"Congratulations." I stood and gave him a hug.

"Thanks! Oh, watch the arm." He jerked away and resituated an icepack he had strapped to his shoulder.

I released my arms and was glad that his reaction to my touch didn't offend my heart. Maybe God had answered my prayers after all. "Sorry, I should have hugged you from the other side."

"You played so well!" Collin's mom, Suzanne, stepped in front of me and I took a step back, giving her room.

"Great job, Son." Pastor Clifton shook Collin's hand. I took a seat in the booth, allowing them to have their family moment because it was obvious I really didn't belong. Collin's little brother, Shane, high-fived him and I smiled, knowing that he'd be a great ballplayer one day, too.

My mom and dad hugged Luke, telling him he did a good job, even though his team lost. He shrugged off their compliment and I sensed he was disappointed in the way he played. The guys slid into the booth and I was surprised that Delaney stayed seated next to me instead of trying to sit next to Luke. I appreciated that was she was adhering to her promise of staying by my side to support me. They eyed each other as though transferring their secret love language to one another.

"You played well, Luke," I said, disrupting their soulful gaze.

"No." He shook his head. "I really didn't. That's why we lost."

"No, it's not." Forbes grabbed a plate and handed it to Jordan.

"Thank you, pumpkin," Jordan replied. She served herself a slice of pizza and then handed Forbes the pie cutter.

"I screwed up too, missing several fly balls." Forbes stacked a few pieces on his plate and then licked his fingers.

Luke took the pie cutter from Forbes and cut a large slice. "I guess the white team didn't have their shit together tonight. Wait until Friday night." Luke pointed to Collin with the spatula. "We're going to kick y'all's asses."

"Yeah, right." Collin laughed. "We'll see about that."

The guys ranted about who would win and I drifted off, thinking of how I wanted to start the conversation with Collin once we were alone. No matter how many times I had rehearsed it, it changed every time. The more I thought about it, the more nervous I got. Minutes prior, I had felt confident and reassured with my decision. I wasn't sure what had caused my shift, but I was becoming a nervous wreck. I picked at my pizza and sipped on my soda, but nothing could unwind the ball of nerves wrapped tightly around my stomach. I watched the clock on the wall and with each passing minute, I convinced myself I could do it.

"You all right, Lexi?" Jordan asked, breaking my daze.

"Huh?" I eased the straw from my mouth.

"You haven't eaten one bite of your pizza." She pointed to my plate.

"Oh, um... I'm not feeling—"

"Hey kids, we're leaving. It's almost eleven and your dad has to get up early." Mom squeezed Luke in a hug and kissed him on the cheek. I elbowed Delaney, delighted that my parents would soon have someone else to hound instead of me.

"It's not me that you need to worry about," I whispered, feeling a little relief flow over me.

She sipped on her empty glass, slurping through the straw until nothing was left. I assumed the stories of my parents overbearing and controlling nature set off an alert in her head.

"Okay, thanks for coming to support me." Luke pried himself from Mom's arms and then shook Dad's hand.

"Bye." I waved, glad that I was sandwiched in between Collin and Delaney. Even though another hug from Dad would have been nice and might have calmed my frazzled nerves, I sacrificed just to stay away from my mom.

Collin shook my parents' hands. "Mr. Thompson, Mrs. Thompson."

"Call me, Mom, it won't be long now." Mom placed her hand on top of Collin's and smiled from ear to ear.

A whimper escaped my throat and everyone turned and looked at me.

Oh, shit.

"Is everything okay?" Collin asked.

I swallowed hard as the words failed me. I knew what I had to do, but it wasn't the right time. We needed to be alone.

"Lexi?"

Delaney gave me a slight nudge and I blurted, "No."

He withdrew his hand and looked at me. "What's wrong?"

I stared at him for a few seconds, telling myself I had to do it. I had to tell him. I couldn't put off the conversation one more day. A cold sweat broke from my skin and the palpitations coming from the center of my chest told me I had to be having a heart attack. I looked around, wondering if there was a defibrillator hanging on the wall somewhere because I knew I was going to need it. "We have to talk."

"Okay." Collin gave a soft shake of his head.

"Sweetie, it's kind of late. Why don't we drop you off at your dorm and you can talk to Collin tomorrow," Mom spoke up. "Delaney, would you like a ride back?"

"Um..." Delaney leaned against me, pushing me to get out of the booth.

For a moment, I wasn't sure what she wanted me to do, but I refused to let my mom get in the way of my plans.

"No, Mom, we don't need a ride back." I pushed on Collin until he slid out of the booth. "We need to talk now," I said in a calm and deliberate tone.

"Is something wrong?" Pastor Clifton and Suzanne walked up behind my parents. They looked at me and then at Collin. Did everyone have to get in our business?

"Lexi said she needs to talk to Collin, but since it's late, we're taking her to the dorm," Dad informed them, looking me straight in the eye.

"Okay." Pastor Clifton turned to his son. "We can drop you off if you like."

"No!" I grabbed Collin by the hand and pushed past our parents. They wouldn't stop me from doing what I had to do.

Not tonight.

Not ever.

"Collin, we have to talk now."

"Lexi, stop." Collin pulled on my hand and I stumbled back. "Your dad is right. It's late and we can talk tomorrow."

"No, this can't wait." I shook my head. I knew that if I didn't tell him, I might not ever have the courage to tell him. I'd live in regret for the rest of my life.

With an incredulous stare, Collin said, "What is wrong with you? You're acting crazy again."

I ran my fingers through my hair, gathering clumps of it in my fist. Maybe I was going crazy. Maybe I needed to be committed or see a therapist. All I knew was that the longer I kept myself within this controlling circle, I would truly go insane. "This wedding is driving me crazy. Your parents are driving me crazy and so are mine." My eyes darted to his parents and then to my family.

Mom covered her mouth as she gasped. Dad's eyes bulged to the point the whites took over and his light skin turned a blistering red.

"Excuse me?" Pastor Clifton cocked his head to the side and Suzanne blinked rapidly as she drew a hand to her chest.

"I'm sorry, but I can't do this." I released my hair and crossed my arms over my body, supporting myself the best way I knew how.

"Do what?" Collin's brows knitted together.

With a steady, low voice, I replied, "Marry you." As I released the air in my lungs, the blocks of pressure exploded, vanishing as they crumbled one by one, in a fast, sweeping action.

I had done it.

And it felt so damn good.

My hands shook, but I managed to pull my engagement ring off my finger. Without looking at it, I reached for Collin's hand and placed it in the center of his palm.

                                  CM Doporto

Collin stared at the band for a few seconds and then looked up at me. The muscles in his arms became rigid and his brows narrowed as his forehead creased. What was he thinking? I had to know. I searched his face, waiting to see if he would give me a sign. The center and outer layers of his eyes clouded over and all traces of emotions vanished. Once again, Collin remained unaffected by what I had just told him.

His lips parted and a flash of hope struck me. I kept my eyes steady on his, waiting anxiously for him to speak, but he kept silent. Why did he continue to hold back from me? After all these years, why wouldn't he let me in? Was it that damn hard to tell me how he felt?

I couldn't understand why he was so afraid to share his feelings with me. Even though part of me was glad the wedding was off, another part wanted him to take me in his arms and show me the love he'd been repressing all these years. I waited for him to say something, anything. But he said nothing.

Nothing at all.

I pressed my trembling lips together as tears poured down my face. I continued waiting, hoping it was just shock that stole his words. After several long minutes, I was convinced that he had nothing to say. I didn't know if it was from lack of caring or relief, but my guess was that he didn't want to get married either. He just didn't know how to tell me.

"We're not in love, Collin." I wiped the tears from my face. "We're nothing but friends. I can't marry someone who's afraid to tell me and, more than that, *show me* they love me."

He looked down at his hand one more time before closing it and dropping it to his side. "Is this what you really want?"

I felt my heart split in two along with my body as it internally crumbled to the floor. Delaney was right. It did hurt. It hurt so damn bad because I had hoped that he would tell me I was wrong.

That he couldn't live without me.

That he needed me.

That he loved me more than anything.

But he didn't.

His response confirmed what we both knew. We didn't love each other enough to get married.

"Lexi, don't do this," Mom pleaded.

I sighed and with the energy I had left, turned toward my parents. "I'm sick and tired of doing what you want. My entire life I have followed every rule you set, adhered to your expectations, learned to withhold myself and do without the things that I wanted most." I took in a deep breath. "Well, I'm done. I can't live like this any longer. I don't need either of you to watch over me, including Luke or Collin. I'm a grown woman and I will do whatever the hell I please."

Mom gasped and Dad's jaw tightened. They looked at the Norris's and quickly averted their stare back to me. I knew I had embarrassed them, but I couldn't take one more second, minute, hour, or day under their restraints. I was tired of living to please them. I needed to live for me.

I turned my gaze back to Collin. "So that's it? You have nothing else to say?"

His shoulders slumped and he grabbed on to the edge of the booth. "What do you want me to say?"

The room spun and my body heaved forward. Four years of giving my life to him and he had nothing to say. His failure to respond answered every question I had. He didn't love me enough to marry me. Collin's decision was clear. He didn't want me in his life and he sure didn't want me to be his wife.

Σ

Chapter 14

"Lex, get up. You're not staying one more day in this bed." Delaney flipped on the light and yanked the sheets off me. The brightness behind my lids made me squeeze my eyes tighter. For the past month, I'd grown accustomed to the dark. That's where I found comfort.

"Stop," I moaned. "I'm sick and need to sleep."

"You're not sick," she huffed. "Maybe sick in the head but that's it. Now, get up..."

Grabbing a pillow, I covered my face and ignored her rambling.

I had lied to everyone, including my parents, telling them I had the flu so I wouldn't have to go home for Thanksgiving break. My dad's brother and family were coming into town and they agreed to let me stay at the dorm since it was open during the holidays. Mom didn't want me passing my sickness to everyone, even though that wouldn't have happened because I really didn't have the flu. Lucky for me, I looked like a zombie from *The Walking Dead* when she showed up with cans of soup and juice, and she believed me.

"Why are you here? Aren't you supposed to be at the farm?" I mumbled against the fabric.

"I came to check on you. And boy, I'm glad I did." She shuffled around my room, but I didn't care to see what she was doing.

"I'm fine, so you can go home." It was a lie because the break with Collin had left me feeling lifeless and cold. I soon discovered my freedom was a lonely world. Part of me was glad to not be marrying him, but I didn't know how to mend my heart back together. I was convinced it was beyond repair. I was fine if I never found love.

"No, you're not!" She pulled the pillow away from my face. "You look like death!" She sniffed the air. "And smell like it, too."

"Good, maybe I'm dying." I rolled over and pulled myself in to a fetal position.

"If you're that miserable, why don't you go back to Collin?"

"Uh, no, that's not an option." I had spent the last month convincing myself that I had done the right thing. I avoided him at all costs, even to the point of taking an incomplete in my Spanish class. My parents were of no help either and I did my best to stay away from them. To my surprise, my dad supported me, but my mother lectured me weekly and refused to let it go. Luckily, my brother told me it was between Collin and me and he wanted no part of it. And, since my sister never bothered to call me, she was one less person I had to worry about.

"Then why are you so upset?"

I reached for a bottle of soda on my nightstand and took a drink. "Ugh, that's flat."

She grabbed the nearly empty bottle from me. "How old is this?"

"I don't know." I shrugged. "A few days."

"Gross."

I turned away from her and fell against my pillow.

"Well, get up and take a shower because we're going to the game."

I stifled a laugh. "I don't feel like taking a shower and I'm sure as hell not going to the game."

"It's the last game of the year." Her voice lilted and I tried hard not to let that yearning deep inside of me get excited.

"Good," I mumbled.

Seeing Raven would not be smart. After splitting up with Collin, I had called Dr. Phillips and told him I quit. I blamed it on personal issues, which was true. He immediately asked if it had anything to do with Raven, but I told him no, even though it partially did. For one entire week, Raven had sent me text messages, begging to know why I wouldn't be tutoring him any longer. I ignored every one of his text and refused to see him when he showed up at my dorm.

"You have to go." Delaney opened my closet door and started rummaging through my clothes.

"No, I don't." I threw a pillow at her. "I told you I'm not going anywhere."

Taking out a pair of my skinny jeans, she said, "That's a damn shame because Raven sent you tickets for the game."

"Shut up." I shot straight up in my bed. "No he didn't." The familiar pounding in the center of my chest returned, only this time it stuttered like a car on the brink of breaking down.

"Yes, he did." She reached into her back pocket and pulled out two tickets.

"Let me see those," I demanded.

She handed me a shiny index-sized card with a football player on the front. The stub indicated the seats were located on the Championship Level. When I saw the sticker price, I knew she couldn't have bought them. They had to be from Raven. The rattling in my chest continued as it tried to find the right rhythm.

"And wear this." She threw my jeans and a shirt at me.

I picked up the oversized, purple, silky shirt, fumbling to catch a better glimpse of it. On the front was the number six stitched in a white reptile-looking print. I flipped it over and ran my hand across the lettering on the back that spelled 'Davenport'. "Where did you get this?"

She smiled and then flopped on to my bed. "He gave it to me."

"What? When?"

She rolled over on to her stomach and propped herself up on her elbows. "About fifteen minutes ago."

"He came here again?" I jumped out of bed and held the jersey up to me. It was a little big and I knew it wasn't one he had worn, but it definitely had his number and name on the back. It also smelled like him, replacing the funky smell in my room. "What did he say?"

"He said he wanted me to take you to the game."

"No he didn't." I eyed her, trying to determine if she was lying to me or if this was one of her scams. For the past few weeks, she continued to encourage me to get out and live my life. She had invited me to go out with her and Jordan, but I continuously turned her down. And every time she brought up Raven, I stopped her from going any further. This wasn't the first time she had tried to convince me to go see him.

"I swear." She held up her hands in surrender. "He said to make sure you wore his jersey so he could find you."

My blood quickened through my veins, but my fractured heart quickly reminded me that Raven also had an agenda. He wanted to have more fun with me, whatever that meant. I shook my head, refusing to listen to the voice telling me to go. It was too soon to hang out with him. My heart needed more time to heal.

"Whatever." I tossed the jersey at her and she caught it mid-air.

"Damn, what's it going to take for you to believe me?"

"Okay. I believe you." I opened my dresser and took out a clean bra and panties. "Do I need to remind you that you told me not to get involved with him?"

"No I didn't." She threw the jersey back at me and I lunged forward to catch it. "I said to be careful. Besides, the poor guy really thinks he did something wrong. You at least need to talk to him."

"What do you mean he thinks he did something wrong? What exactly did he say?" I asked, wary.

"Umm... well, I kind of told him what happened between you and Collin and that—"

"You did what?" The muscles in my hands tensed and I balled them into fists.

"I'm sorry." Delaney pressed her hands together, pleading for forgiveness. "I felt sorry for him. He thought what happened at the stadium suite, which wasn't much, made you mad." I had confided in Delaney about the heated situation at the football stadium a few days after I called off the marriage. I had confessed to her that I had never told him I was engaged because it never came up. I also hadn't offered to tell him.

"Oh." Covering my face with my clean clothes, I moaned. "I can't believe you told him." There really wasn't a reason he needed to know about Collin. I had no plans of starting up something with him. Everything I felt for Raven was just hyped up because of what I wanted and longed for from Collin, at least that's what I had told myself for the past month. It didn't help the fact that I was silently dying to see him.

"He would have found out eventually."

I lowered my hands. "How?"

"Things get around." She waved her hand in the air.

"Maybe about you, but not about me."

"Ouch!" Delaney pretended to stab herself in the chest with her fist.

"Sorry." I let the anger go because what was done, was done.

"Anyhow, he invited us to a party tonight." Holding up her phone, she showed me her Facebook page.

I grabbed the phone from her and stared at the invite. "You're friends with Raven?" My mouth fell open. "Hell, I'm not even friends with him." A spiral of jealously hit me. Why was she trying to be friends with him? She needed to worry about Luke, not about Raven.

"I'm friends with a lot of guys. Even those I don't sleep with, so get over it. And don't worry; I don't want to sleep with Raven. I actually prefer your brother." She smiled and her face glowed.

"If you say so." I watched for a moment and the glint in her eyes told me she was sincere.

Slowly, she eased the phone from my hands. "Besides, how often are you on Facebook?"

"Umm... I don't know..."

"Exactly. Never." Placing my jeans in my arms, she got up from the bed and shuffled me to the bathroom. "Get dressed, the clock is ticking."

"No." I shook my head, still fighting the inevitable.

"Oh, come on, you know you want to go." She turned on the shower and backed out of the bathroom, closing the door behind her.

I placed my clothes on the counter and wiped the steam from the mirror. I didn't like who I had become. I hadn't done any of the things I had told my parents and Collin. Why wasn't I living my life? There was no one to stop me or tell me I couldn't do any of it. I was free to do what I wanted. Yet, I had done nothing. A smile crept up over my face and I quickly pulled off the clothes I had been wearing for the past week. It was time to start living my life for me.

"Holy crap, Delaney! These have to be the best seats in the house." I stared in awe, taking in the field that was only a few feet in front of us on the fifty-yard line. The bright green grass contrasted against the canvas of purple and white that spread from top to bottom in the stadium, drowning the opposing team's colors of gold and green. Dance music blared over the speakers as the coaches, referees, and other personnel rushed along the sideline, preparing for the game to start.

"Do you think he owns these seats?" Delaney waved to a group of people behind us that I didn't know. "Hey! What's up?"

"I doubt it. Someone probably gave him the tickets." I looked around, wondering if Raven's mother and brothers were nearby. Since I had never met them, I had no idea if they were there. An older lady and man shuffled past us and sat in the empty seats next to me. Based on their blondish hair color and fair skin, I knew they weren't his family. Raven had a creamy, light brown skin color and dark hair indicating he was probably a mixed race. Maybe Hispanic or African American with some Anglo. Whatever his parents were, it made him one damn hot guy.

"It probably works the same way it does for baseball. They designate certain seats for the players and their family."

Pressing my fingers to my temples, I closed my eyes. I didn't want to think about Collin.

"Sorry, didn't mean to bring that up."

After pushing him to the furthest recesses of my mind, I opened my eyes. "It's okay."

The sun was directly overhead and warmed the air to a nice sixty-five degrees, proving it would be a great day for football. A train horn blared and smoke filled the south end zone. The big screen flickered with lights and the announcer spoke over the loud speaker. The game was starting. The people around us stood and immediately began clapping as the spirit team entered the field, carrying large purple flags that spelled PHU. Delaney and I joined the crowd, cheering as the football team made their grand entrance. The band played as guys in black jerseys and tight spandex pants with chrome purple helmets sprinted across the turf. I scanned through all of them, looking for Raven.

"There he is!" Delaney pointed. "Almost in the center of the field."

His number called to me, drawing my eyes directly to him.

"Yep, that's him." I pressed my lips together, holding back a smile that fought to release itself. Seeing him brought back all the memories, especially the most vivid one that took place in the stadium several weeks prior. There was no denying what I felt with him and what I was experiencing in that moment. A silent calling that moved my body, shaking it to the core.

I watched him track to the side in front of the forty-yard line along with several other players as they waited for the referee to start the game. He huddled with several of his teammates and appeared to be reviewing plays. A whistle blew and the players clapped their hands before breaking apart and running to their positions on the field. Raven looked into the stands and I immediately raised my hands in the air. "Raven! Raven!"

His eyes searched the crowd. When he noticed me, he pointed a finger at me and winked.

I pointed at his jersey I had on and a huge smiled covered his face. I smiled back, glad that I had decided to go to the game. I couldn't fight my desire to want to be with him. It was strong and forceful, propelling me toward him once again. I released the breath I was holding and prayed that I was doing the right thing, even though my head warned me it was too soon.

Delaney elbowed me. "And you didn't want to come."

With a slight roll of my eyes, I said, "I know. I know."

"Did she just wave to Raven?" A voice dripping with jealously whispered and I cringed. The girl who said the comment was directly behind us. She either had a thing for Raven or knew someone who did. I reminded myself of whom Raven was and that there was no way to escape the world he had created around him. Did I really want to be a part of that world? I eased into my seat, ignoring the remark.

"Hmm. Whatever," the girl continued, as though waiting for me to turn around and say something.

Delaney tucked her phone in the inside of her boot and leaned close to me. "Did that girl behind us just say something about you?"

"Yeah, I think so," I whispered.

"Don't worry. She ain't got nothing on you," another girl spoke. I inched down in my chair. I didn't think wearing the jersey would have drawn attention to me, but apparently it had.

"I shouldn't have come." I frowned when I heard a slew of laughter bellow from their high-pitched voices. It reverberated through my ears, reminding me of the types of girls he was known for hooking up with.

"That's it." Delaney sat her drink in the cup holder and flung around.

"No! Don't." I grabbed her arm and tried to stop her, but she pulled away.

"Do y'all have a problem?" Delaney stood with her hands on her hips, eyeing the three voluptuous girls behind us.

Great.

I stood to get a better view of whom my new enemies were. A girl with dark, wavy hair and long, tanned legs reclined in her seat, ignoring Delaney. She wore a tight baby doll T-shirt with Raven's number on it.

Perfect. Another one of his hoes.

The two other girls sitting next to her giggled and then looked away. One of them stared at their fingernails, admiring her purple and white nail polish, while the other one played with her long, blonde waves as she stared into the crowd with a clueless expression. They were all so pitiful looking that I couldn't help but shake my head.

"Because if you do, you know you can leave." Delaney stood her ground, waiting until they caught her gaze. I gripped the edge of my seat, praying that these girls wouldn't want to fight. I knew that Delaney wouldn't have thought twice about hitting them, but I would've been useless, having never fought a day in my life.

"I'm sorry, did you say something?" The long-legged brunette cocked her head to the side, feigning ignorance. The other girls continued to ignore Delaney and I was confident they wouldn't want to mess up their pretty hair and nails. I took in a deep breath and allowed my shoulders to relax. Raven was right. I really was an upgrade in comparison to those ditzy hoes. I had no reason to feel inferior to any of them. They might have had bigger lips and boobs than me, but I was glad to be silicone free. Even though I was in the peewee league, I knew that I could learn what I needed to know to advance me.

If only I had the courage to do it.

"Forget about it, Laney, they're not worth wasting our breaths over." I placed my hand on her shoulder and turned us around just in time to see Raven score a touchdown. The stadium erupted in to applause and the train horn blared. Raven high fived his team mates and did a little dance across the end zone.

"All right, Raven!" I yelled, not afraid to show those skanks and everyone else whom I supported. After all, he was the reason I had come to the game.

To my relief, the girls sitting behind us left with a few frat guys during half time and never came back. I assumed they had lured them into their hoe-trap and went to take care of business. I was glad they were gone because it made the game more enjoyable, especially when Raven threw the winning touchdown. We waited until the players cleared the field and then followed the remaining crowd out of the stadium.

"That really was a good game, despite those stupid biotches nearly ruining it for us." Delaney pushed her way through the herds of people, dragging me along with her. "I thought I was going to have to plant my boot in their pretty little faces."

"I know," I huffed as I dodged a group of guys painted in purple without shirts.

"Damn! Can't you wait?" Delaney yelled as she stumbled to catch her footing.

"They're probably drunk."

We wiggled our way through the congested walkways until we were able to squeeze through the gates that led to the front of the stadium.

"Whew." Delaney fanned herself. "I hate being that close to people. I'm so glad the base—I was thinking we should probably go to the store and buy some Coke. We can mix our own drinks before the party tonight."

I stopped, causing the people walking behind me to make a trail around me. Delaney looked over her shoulder when she realized I wasn't following her.

She tracked back toward me. "What's wrong?"

Keeping my eyes trained to the ground, I said, "I don't know. After what happened in the stands, I'm not sure I should go. "

"Don't be silly—"

"Hey, Delaney, great game, huh?" A cute guy with spiky blond hair and a tight Kappa Sigma T-shirt stepped in front of us. Two of his friends waved at her as they darted across the parking lot to a huge white tent with their fraternity's name on it.

Delaney smiled, giving a small wave and then tucked a strand of her hair behind her ear. "Definitely. We kicked the Bears right in the ass."

The guy laughed and then shoved his hands in his pant pockets. "Why don't you come on over?" He motioned to the tailgate party that was happening at the tent. "We're starting the party early."

She pressed her lips together and looked around as though checking to see if Luke was anywhere around. I could tell that being around this guy made her really nervous. "Yeah, I don't know. Um—"

"Delaney! Are you going tonight?" A girl with curly blonde hair wearing a short purple dress and cowboy boots rushed toward us. The girls that were with her headed straight for the tailgate party. It seemed like everyone was going to this pre-party except for us.

"I'll see ya later?" The guy tilted his head to the side, trying to get her attention.

"Um, yeah." She nodded and then turned to her friend.

"Shelby, what happened to you? I saw you in the stands and then I couldn't find you."

Her long eyelashes fanned across her painted lids and when she smiled, two little balls formed at the top of her cheeks. She resembled Anna Sophia Robb from the Carrie Diaries. "Oh, Josh's parents have a suite, so I went up there to join them." She turned toward me. "Hi, I'm Shelby Scott."

"Oh, sorry." Delaney thumped her forehead with her hand. "This is my roommate, Lexi Thompson."

"Nice to meet you." I shook her hand.

"Come on." Shelby laced her arms through ours as if we had been life-long friends. "Let's go see what's going on with these Kappa Sigs while I wait for Josh."

"Shelby's dating Josh Marshall," Delaney shot me quick glare, "you know, the running back."

I had to be the biggest idiot because aside from Raven, I really didn't know all the players. Then, it dawned on me. That was Raven's friend, Josh. It was his parent's suite we were in when he snuck me into the stadium. "Oh yea, number thirty-seven."

"Yep, that's my guy." She giggled and her blue eyes sparkled. Without even seeing them interact, I was willing to bet they were one happy couple. I waited for that familiar pain to return to the center of my chest, finding myself surprised when it didn't come. Had my heart grown that cold? Or was it so broken that it forgot how to feel?

Shelby introduced Delaney and me to her girlfriends and in turn, they introduced us to their boyfriends that were all Kappa Sigs. Delaney managed to stay away from the cute blond guy and I made it a point to ask about him later.

"Drink anyone?" Shelby appeared with two red Solo cups in hand.

"Sure." Delaney took the cup and immediately took a sip.

"Thanks. What is it?" I stared into the orange Kool-Aid looking liquid.

"I don't know." She shrugged as she picked up her drink from the bed of one of the trucks backed up to the tent.

"Taste like Gatorade mixed with Vodka, if you ask me." Delaney swirled her drink around.

I laughed. "Seriously?"

"Yep, I think you're right." Shelby rolled her tongue across her lips. "I see you're wearing Raven's number. Do you know him or are ya just a fan?" Shelby eyed my jersey while sipping on her drink.

Delaney shot me a quick glance.

"Um..." I bit down on my lip and wondered what to tell her. There wasn't anything to hide since I was no longer engaged, but I wasn't sure if I wanted to share my business, especially with someone I barely knew. If I planned on going to the party, people would see me talking to him. What the hell.

"I know him and I'm also a fan," I openly admitted.

"Oh." Her brows lifted as she took a drink. "Raven and my boyfriend, Josh, are roommates."

"Really? I didn't know that." She probably thought I was hoping to get a chance with him, like every other girl. Sadly, that description kind of fit me in a twisted sort of way. The more I tried to convince myself that I had no business getting involved with him, the more I wanted to.

"I'm sorry. I don't mean to be rude. It's just that I've never seen you around before." Her eyes darted to a group of girls standing in the corner, the Silicone Triplets that were sitting behind us in the stands.

Great.

"It's okay." I smiled at her, assuring her that I didn't take offense to her comment. "We're just friends." I hesitated to tell her too much, but I wanted her to know that I wasn't one of them. "Actually, I was his writing tutor," I leaned forward and whispered, "but don't tell anyone."

"Oh my God!" She pulled her drink away from her mouth, spilling some in the process. "You're the girl?"

"What?" Breathless, I looked at Delaney and she gave me a clueless stare. "What do mean, I'm the girl?"

She pressed her lips together and then let out a breath. "Josh said that Raven mentioned you a few times. That's all."

"Seriously?" My stomach lifted and released the nest of butterflies that had been trapped for the past several weeks. Raven talked about me to his friend? Had he said good things or bad things about me?

"Oh my God." Delaney drew us in closer. "You have to tell us."

"I don't know much." She had a dubious expression, like she was scared to tell us what she knew. It was obvious that she was withholding some vital information.

Information that I was dying to hear.

Information that I had to have.

"Please?" I clamped my hands tighter around my cup, making it pop.

I guessed my pleading made her give in or maybe she felt sorry for me. She quickly traded glances with us and then said, "Well, okay. All I know is that he told Josh he was working with this tutor, which is you," she pointed at me, "that he really liked. He also said she was very pretty and extremely smart."

My mouth fell open and I took a step back. With a hand on my chest, I tried to steady my heavy breathing. "He said that? About me?"

She nodded. "That's what Josh said. Which says a lot because Raven never talks to Josh about girls." She rolled her eyes when the head Silicone Triplet laughed loudly. "At least not ones he really likes, and I mean, *really* likes."

"Oh, wow. That does say lot." Delaney chewed on her nail as though the comments were about her.

"There's my guy!" Shelby held out her arms, welcoming Josh. "Excuse me." She ran to him and jumped into his arms. With her legs and arms wrapped around him, he swung her around. That proved my theory was right about them being in love. It was more than obvious. They kind of reminded me of Forbes and Jordan.

How does one find a guy that doesn't even think twice about showing their girl how much they mean to them?

As they moved to the side, lip locked with each other, I turned and saw Raven stroll into the tent. My body wafted in the air as the butterflies took flight again. I hadn't been that close to him in weeks and my body hummed in delight. I shamelessly took in every inch of his well-defined body. From his damp hair to the jeans that sat low on his waist. My eyes traveled up the ripples of muscles that stretched underneath his purple and white polo style shirt, making my fingers tingle as they remembered what it felt like to hold on to him. The more I remembered, the more I wanted to touch him and never let go.

He caught my gaze and his lips parted into a perfect smile. A smile that warmed every part of me, including my heart, which instantly remembered what it felt like to beat again.

"Hi." He appraised me for a moment, making every muscle and fiber move inside of me. How did he know how to make me move like that?

"Hey." I rose up on the balls of my feet as I wrapped my arms around me. I could have stared at his perfect smile forever. "Great game."

He neared me until we stood face to face. "I'm glad you came."

"I couldn't miss seeing you play your last game of the season." I warded off the heat consuming my cheeks.

"You look good in that jersey." His eyes settled on my chest and I shifted my weight to the side.

"Thanks. Although, some of the girls didn't like that I was wearing it." I glanced over to the Silicone Triplets that were gawking at us.

Raven smirked. "Don't worry about them, okay?" He tucked a stray strand of my hair behind my ear and then dragged his finger along my jawline. Hot and cold shivers spread over my body as it begged for more of his sweet affection.

"Great game, Raven." A guy patted him on the shoulder.

"Thanks, man."

The people around us cheered and congratulated him every few minutes, barely allowing us to talk. Raven thanked them, shook their hands, and even fist-bumped those that supported how he had played. I tried to subdue the happiness that gleamed from me, but I couldn't hold it back.

He shoved his hands in his pockets and whispered in my ear, "Do you want to get out of here?"

Tingles spread from my head to my toes and I froze. Raven was actually asking me if I wanted to leave with him? I waited for every warning light to go off, but only one flashed in my mind.

Trust.

Could I trust him?

I wanted to trust him, but my past interactions with him reminded me that his reputation and actions weren't worthy of my trust. Yet, he hadn't done anything for me not to trust him. The weight of my fear lingered, distorting my mind and making it hard to distinguish what I really wanted. But deep down inside, I knew what I wanted. Biting down on my lip, I nodded, not caring if anyone saw me leave with him.

He took me by the hand and led me through the crowd. The Silicone Triplets huffed and muttered incoherent words as we passed by them. Instead of reacting to their childish remarks, I ignored them. I handed Delaney my cup as we exited the tent. "I'll see you later."

She took the cup and winked at me. "If you don't make it home tonight, I know why."

Raven stopped and turned around. "Hey, I heard that."

Delaney's eyes widened and a look of dread draped over her face. "I didn't—"

"Relax. I'm just messing with you." He grinned and she sighed in relief. Pulling me closer to him, he said, "I promise to bring her home when she tells me."

Holding back a giggle, I waved to her as we crossed the parking lot.

"So, you've been in hiding?" He kept in step with me as we walked toward his car.

I kept my eyes trained to the ground, praying he wouldn't ask me about Collin. I knew I would eventually need to tell him my side of the story, because I had no idea what Delaney had told him, but I wasn't in the mood to talk about it. "I guess you can say that. I was going through some personal stuff."

"I understand." The sincerity in his voice told me he was being truthful. "I'm sorry to, um, hear—"

"It's okay." My stomach tensed and I took a few deep breaths. "It wasn't meant to be."

He unlocked the car door and opened it for me. "Well, I'm here for you if you want to talk or need anything at all."

I swallowed the huge ball of nerves that was working its way out of me. "Thanks, I appreciate it." I got in the car and he shut the door.

It felt good to know that he was willing to listen to me, be there for me. Collin never offered me that. It was so obvious why I couldn't find love with him. I wondered if he was discovering the same thing. I refused to ask Luke if Collin had confided in him about us. I just wanted to move on with my life and being with Raven was allowing me to do that.

Raven slid into the front seat and shut the door. We sat there for a moment in silence. The sun was beginning to set, spreading hues of pink and purple across the sky. With one arm resting on the steering wheel and the other on the console between us, he turned to me.

"Can I be honest with you?"

I pivoted in my seat, facing him. "Sure, as long as I can be honest with you."

We exchanged a silent agreement as our gaze drew us closer together. My eyes searched his face, carefully examining every detail from the defined arch in his brows to the scar on his right cheekbone that disappeared in his slight five o'clock shadow. I watched as his eyes scanned over me and then rested on my lips.

Lifting his eyes, he stared deep into mine. "I've really missed seeing you."

My heart pounded, telling me it was well on its way to mending. I swallowed back the fear that replayed over and over in my head.

Could I really trust him?

Not wanting to regret one passing moment with him, I tossed the fear aside and told him how I really felt. "I've missed you, too."

"Do you remember what I told you in the suite?" His eyes shifted up toward the stadium for a quick second and then returned to me. His look unraveled me, leaving me defenseless against his trap.

Was I ready for The Raven's trap?

I was slipping effortlessly into it and knew there was no escaping it.

Then again, I didn't want to.

"You told me lots of things."

He inclined his head and then rubbed his chin. "I'm referring to the point I made about me not doing anything unless you asked me to."

"Oh, that point." I dropped my hand on the console and inched my fingers closer to his. "Yeah, I remember."

Our fingers brushed against each other and then interlaced. The roughness of his skin against mine sent an instant razzing sensation up my arm. I hesitated for a moment and then said, "Raven, can I ask you to do something?"

He rubbed his thumb back and forth across my flesh, rendering my arm useless. "That depends on what it is." His eyes lit up and I hoped he knew what I wanted him to do.

"Will you kiss me?"

"I thought you'd never ask."

Σ

To Be Continued
The Same Side
Book Two of the University Park Series

From Best Selling Author
CM DOPORTO

THE SAME SIDE

UNIVERSITY PARK SERIES BOOK 2

About the Author

CM Doporto

Born and raised in the United States of America in the great state of Texas, CM Doporto resides there with her husband and son, enjoying life with their extensive family along with their Chihuahua and several fish. She is a member of Romance Writers of America, where she is associated with the Young Adult Special Interest Chapter. To learn more about her upcoming books, visit www.cmdoporto.com and sign up to receive email notifications. You can also like CM Doporto's fan page on Facebook and follow her on Instagram, Twitter and Pinterest.

Other Books by
<u>CM Doporto</u>

YOUNG ADULT

The Eslite Chronicles

The Eslites (short story prequel)

The Eslites, The Arrival

The Eslites, Out of This World (Summer 2015)

NEW ADULT

The Natalie Vega Saga

Element, Part 1

Element, Part 2

The University Park Series

Opposing Sides

The Same Side

The Winning Side

A Different Side (Coming Soon)

My Lucky Catch (Summer 2015) - Luke and Delaney's Story

Made in the USA
San Bernardino, CA
08 July 2015